Eystein Asgrimsson

Lilja

Salzwasser

Eystein Asgrimsson

Lilja

1. Auflage | ISBN: 978-3-84605-056-9

Erscheinungsort: Frankfurt, Deutschland

Erscheinungsjahr: 2020

Salzwasser Verlag GmbH

Reprint of the original, first published in 1870.

LILJA

(THE LILY)

AN ICELANDIC RELIGIOUS POEM OF THE FOURTEENTH CENTURY.

BY

EYSTEIN ÁSGRIMSSON

REGULAR OF THE MONASTERY OF THYKKVIBŒR.

EDITED, WITH A METRICAL TRANSLATION, NOTES, AND GLOSSARY,

BY

EIRIKR MAGNUSSON,

TRANSLATOR OF
'LEGENDS OF ICELAND,' 'THE SAGA OF GUNNLAUG THE WORMTONGUE,'
'GRETTIS SAGA.' 'VÖLSUNGA.' ETC.

1870.

CONTENTS.

PREFACE.

THE Lily all bards would fain have sung, 'öll skáld vildu Lilju kveðið hafa,' is the short and pithy award which Iceland accords to the following song. I have explained (p. xlix) how I am not able to introduce it in its sonorous graces to the English reader; but I have given him all aid in my power towards the realisation of them, by the explanation of the sounds of the Icelandic letters, and the metre: which, although an unsatisfactory aid, is still better than nothing. The manner in which my work is done needs no explanation here. Any one desirous of satisfying himself on that point will find no difficulty in forming an *independent* opinion on the subject by the aid of the Introduction, the Translation, the Notes, and the Glossary.

In a bibliographical point of view it may interest some readers to know that the present is the first Icelandic text which has ever been published in England itself from manuscript sources.

As to the rest, let the work speak for itself.

EIRIKR MAGNUSSON.

London, September 1870.

INTRODUCTION.

I.

Notice of the Life of the Author.

EYSTEIN ASGRIMSSON—Brother Eystein, as he is commonly called—was an Icelander by birth, an Augustinian friar by profession. His early life is wrapped in thorough darkness, and his latter days only glimmer here and there through a general mist of uncertainties. We know that he lived in the earlier half of the fourteenth century; but our knowledge of his life, long or short as it may have been, extends only to the latter eighteen years of it, through which period we can trace him by stray notices of chroniclers, contemporary documents, and legendary tradition.

The life of Eystein has not been written before. Notices of him may be found in Bishop Finn Jónsson's 'Historia Ecclesiastica Islandiæ,' Havniæ, 1772–78; in Finn Magnússon's observations accompanying his Danish translation of 'Lilja' in Liunge's 'Dana, Poetisk Lommebog for 1818,' a work which I have not seen; and in Espolin's 'Arbœkur Islands, Kaupmannahöfn, 1821–55.' The sources whence nearly all information on record concerning him is to be drawn are 'Annálar Islands,

Kaupmannahöfn, 1847.' The fragmentary information to be gleaned from these authorities I have tried to bring here together into an intelligible order, as well as their disjointed condition would allow.

Brother Eystein's historical career opens with an unpleasant scene. A regular of the monastery of Thykkvibœr,[1] we find him, in 1342, involved, with a couple of accomplices, in an assault upon the abbot of the establishment, Thorlak Loptsson,[2] whom they handled so roughly that he had to fly for his safety, and take shelter in the far distant monastery of Viðey.[3] It is not known what complications actually gave rise to this quarrel, but, from what followed, it may safely be inferred, that it was brought about by zealous reproofs levelled by the abbot at the lax morals of the community. For when, in the following year, the new bishop of the diocese, Jón Sigurdsson (Bishop of Skálholt, 1343–48), took the matter in hand, he found himself justified in warranting the arrest of the

[1] This monastery, founded 1168 by a wealthy magnate, Thorkel Geirisson (ob. 1187), was situate in the district of Skaptafellsþing in the East of Iceland. It often occurs under the parochial denomination of 'The Minster in Ver,' or 'Alptaver,' *i.e.* Swanshaunts. The first abbot of it was Thorlak Thorhallsson, a student of Paris and Lincoln, Bishop of Skalholt, 1178–93, and after his death a saint of the Icelandic Church. It was dissolved in 1551.

[2] Abbot of the monastery, 1314–51. He was declared a saint after his death, and translated in 1360.

[3] *Hist. Eccl.* iv. 60; *Annals*, p. 260.—The convent of Viðey, instituted 1226, was an Augustinian establishment, situate on an island of that name, within the district of Kjalarnes-þing, about six miles from the present capital of Iceland. Bishop Sigurdsson abolished the Augustinian and introduced the Benedictine rule in this monastery 1344, but his successor re-established the Augustinian rite there 1352. This monastery, the first that succumbed to the rapacious Danish reformation, was dissolved in 1542.

ringleaders, among whom the *Annals* assign to Brother Eystein a position of unenviable prominence, and having them arraigned, handcuffed and shackled, before the tribunal of the Church, which, having proved them guilty of immorality and serious misdemeanour, committed them to prison.

According to Bishop Jónsson, Brother Eystein was released from his prison this very year (1343), but on what grounds does not appear.[4] Out of prison, he is said to have betaken himself to Helgafell,[5] another house of his order, where it is likely he sojourned during the next six or seven years, in which no mention is made of him.

The see of Skálholt having become vacant in 1348, by the death of the aforesaid Bishop Sigurdsson, Brother Eystein was selected from among the clergy to perform the duties of an 'Officialis'[6]—a title also given in Iceland to one who acts as vicar during an episcopal vacancy—and in the discharge of these functions we find him from 1349 to 1351, when the new bishop, Gyrd Ivarsson (1349–60), took possession of the chair. This prelate, formerly an abbot of St. John's, Bergen, was nominated to the see already in 1349, and consecrated the following year, but was prevented from leaving Norway on account of the fearful plague which, during these years, devastated the whole

[4] *Hist. Eccl.* i. 587.—Bishop Jónsson knows that his release was effected either by penitence or sufficient fine, which is obvious in itself, but of which I have failed to find any other record.

[5] *Hist. Eccl.* l.c.—This Augustine monastery was originally founded by Bishop Klæng of Skálholt, 1172, on the island of Flatey, situate in the broad bay, called Breiðifjörðr, which cuts into western Iceland. Twelve years afterwards it was moved by Bishop Thorlak to Helgafell, a farmstead on Thorsnes, on the south side of the bay. It was dissolved in 1550.

[6] *Annals*, 282.

of Europe, having interrupted communication between Iceland and Norway for at least a year.[7] In maintaining that Eystein filled the post of 'Officialis' during the vacancy, I am at variance with other writers on the subject.[8] Bishop Jónsson ignores the fact altogether, asserting that nothing is known as to how he may have conducted himself from the time he was released from prison until 1353.[9] But some one must have been appointed Official at the death of Bishop Sigurdsson, and the *Annals* mention Brother Eystein alone in discharge of that function in 1349, and there is every probability in favour of his having continued in the office until the arrival of the new bishop in 1351 ; indeed, his subsequent connection with Bishop Gyrd seems clearly to indicate it, and I have, therefore, no hesitation in maintaining that he was Official from 1349 to 1351.—This great change in Brother Eystein's relation to the church seems to go a long way to prove that his conduct, subsequent to his release from prison, must have been of a nature completely to obliterate all recollection of the stigma which the Thykkvibœr scandal had attached to his name, and that now his character was thoroughly re-established in the eyes of the chapter of the diocese.

Bishop Gyrd, a Norwegian by birth and education, a stranger to the clergy, and ignorant, of course, of the laws, customs, and manners which obtained in his diocese,

[7] *Hist. Eccl.* ii. 102 ; *Annals*, 282.

[8] Except Mr. Jón Thorkelsson in his admirable treatise 'On *r* and *ur* final in Icelandic roots and terminations,' appended to a 'Report of the learned School of Reykjavík, for the School Year 1862–63.' p. 23.

[9] *Hist. Eccl.* i. 587.

was, no doubt, fain to avail himself, on his arrival in Iceland, of the counsel and experience of his able vicar, who, in turn, understood well, we may be certain, how to secure for himself the Bishop's friendship and interest.

In 1353 the Bishop and Brother Eystein made a common cause in the Diet against the prefect of the country, Olaf Bjarnason, in a strife which, though I digress from the straight line of my narrative, I feel bound to treat at some length, as I happen to hold an opinion concerning the relation of the contending parties different from others who have treated the matter.

A certain person, named Guttorm Asgrímsson, had, in company with an accomplice, set at large, illegally, a prisoner from the Prefect's custody. For this he was committed to trial at the Diet, and the court found the criminality of his guilt amounting to that of a capital offence, and sentenced him to death by the axe.[10] This sentence was rigorously executed, as it seems, under the authority of the Prefect—no exercise being allowed of the customary appeal to the royal prerogative of mercy. 'Afterwards,' in the words of the *Annals*, 'sprang up great dispute between the aforesaid Olaf and the Lord Bishop Gyrd and Brother Eystein.'[11] This dispute took its rise evidently from the execution of Guttorm Asgrímsson, and according to the natural construction of the very wording of the passage quoted, the sides were: the Prefect on one, the Bishop and the Brother on the other. A less natural construction would array Prefect and Bishop together against Brother Eystein. But the least natural is the one which Bishop Jónsson follows, grouping Prefect and Eystein on one side, as opposed to the

[10] *Annals*, 284; *Espolin*, i. 84. [11] *Annals*, l.c.; *Espolin*, l.c.

Bishop on the other; for against such arrangement of the contending parties stands the grammatical arrangement of the context, as well as all the evidence of probabilities, the only evidence obtainable in this matter.

In 1353 Bishop Gyrd visited the churches of Rangárvellir, a portion of the eastern diocese of Skálholt. This visitation tour was, in all probability, undertaken at the customary season, after the sitting of the diet was over. I have no means of ascertaining whether Brother Eystein did accompany the Bishop on this tour or not, on account of all original documentary evidence concerning the subject being at present beyond my reach. But from a remark of Bishop Jónsson's about Eystein's signatures *always* occupying the first place among the many venerable names attached to Bishop Gyrd's church deeds,[12] taken together with another observation of his, according to which he makes Eystein quit the country in 1353, bearing also in mind that the above remark cannot apply to any time after 1354, I think it very probable that Eystein was the Bishop's companion on this very visitation tour.

Meanwhile the quarrel which had taken place at the diet did not abate. A meeting, convened for the purpose of settling it, took place at Skálholt on the 22nd of December this same year, where a vague sort of agreement seems to have been arrived at, nominally allaying the contention.[13] But after the meeting the Prefect sailed to Norway with such proofs (in his favour, I presume) as he could procure, which seems to indicate a decided distrust on his part of the solidity of the Skálholt arrangement. I can find no evidence of Eystein having gone abroad this year; but on the 21st of July, the year following,

[12] *Hist. Eccl.* i. 587. [13] *Hist. Eccl.* i. 587.

we find him in Bishop Gyrd's suite in the western portion of the diocese, and his signature occupying the place of honour amongst numerous others, to a deed drawn up for the Church of Fell in Kollafjord, by Bishop Gyrd.[14] For him to have been in Norway between the 22nd of December, 1353, and the 21st of July, 1354, is, of course, possible, but scarcely probable. I am far rather inclined to think that the Brother was all the while an amanuensis to the Bishop, and that they still continued to be fast friends.

One more circumstance in support of this probability. It is held by some historians that Guttorm Asgrímsson was none but Eystein's own brother. And although the proof of it only goes as far as the identity of the paternal name of the two men, that coincidence in a name of no very great preponderance in the nomenclature of personal names in Iceland, is of some weight at all events. Now supposing this to have been the case, it would obviously lead to an alliance of sides such as I maintain it to have been, and would explain naturally the good fellowship of Bishop and Brother in 1353 and 1354. Eystein must necessarily have resorted to the calling in of the powerful aid of the Church, in the person of the Bishop of Skálholt for the reprieving of his relative, if the Prefect persisted in remaining deaf to all his remonstrances. It was in those times a matter of no great difficulty to persuade the Church to assert her authority in cases which concerned her less than the execution of a brother of an ecclesiastic, condemned to death withal by a lay court. The harsh judgment and the hurried execution had in itself nothing to call for interference from the Church, if no weightier interest than outraged justice had been brought to bear. If the culprit

[14] *Hist. Eccl*, ii. 107–108, Espolin mistaken in the date (xii Cal. Aug.) refers it to xii Cal. Jul., 85.

was brother of Eystein, that fact would amount to a conclusive evidence in favour of the supposition, which now I can only maintain as a probability. The historical importance of this point is not a great one, but its interest for the biography of Eystein, of whom we know so little, is very considerable.

Contrary to Bishop Jónsson's assertion that Eystein went to Norway in 1353, I maintain, on the authority of the annals, that he left for Norway in 1355.[15] Arriving out, he betook himself to the Augustinian monastery of Elgisetr (less correctly, Helgisetr) near Drontheim, where he sojourned until 1358. Here he soon gained the good will of the canons of Christ Church Cathedral, Drontheim, and won even the favour of the Archbishop himself. Hence, it may be presumed, it came to pass that in 1357 he was commissioned by the Primate to repair, in company with Canon Brand Eyjólfsson, to Iceland, for the purpose of inquiring into the state of the Icelandic Church.[16] Such visitations which, in pursuance of instructions from Rome, the Metropolitan of Norway, was bound to perform annually throughout his province, he rarely carried out in Iceland.[17] But rare as they had been, they

[15] *Annals*, 288.—Bishop Jónsson's statement, that he had been expelled from his country, *Hist. Eccl.* iv. 34, seems to show that he must have had access to information concerning Eystein's life which now is lost; for no existing records make mention of such an expulsion.

[16] *Hist. Eccl.* i. 562.

[17] Only two such visitations are recorded previous to this time; the first in 1307 on behalf of Archbishop Jörund, his legates being Laurentius Kálfsson, afterwards Bishop of Hólar, and a certain brother Björn, a Dominican from Drontheim; the second had taken place in Eystein's own time (1340), under the authority of Archbishop Paul, his legate being Aslák, a canon of Drontheim. —*Annals*, 190, 256 *Hist. Eccl.* l. c.

had had a thoroughly undesirable effect upon the morals of the Icelandic Church, nor did this one exhibit any redeeming features in that respect.

The commissioners started on their expedition in 1358,[18] visiting first the diocese of Skálholt. An authentic record of their official doings in that diocese still exists, dated the day before Thorlak's mass, 23d December, 1358.[19] It contains, in six articles, an agreement between certain representatives of the clergy and the laity of the diocese, whereby some disputed points concerning the mode of paying tithes and other ecclesiastical dues in various cases were settled; which provisions were to have a binding legal authority, for the diocese of Skálholt, until King and Archbishop, by the counsel of the best men of the realm, should otherwise ordain. This document may be taken fairly to represent the worldly character of the mission, although it does not show it in the same light as the *Annals* seem to do; for from these we gather the impression that no sooner were the legates fairly on their mission in Iceland than deeds of high-handedness and unscrupulous dealings in money matters were loudly complained of. The commissioners were perhaps spurred on in their zeal by the example of the state; for this very year four Prefects had farmed the public revenue of Iceland from the king of Norway, and went over the land exacting money under all sorts of pretences, and fleecing the population wheresoever gold, or gold's worth, was to be obtained. 'Under this,' says the annalist in his plaintive shortness, 'the people of the country had to stand, oppressed as they were by such extortions.'[20]

[18] *Hist. Eccl.* i. 521. [19] *Annals*, 292; *Hist. Eccl.* i. l.c.
[20] *Annals*, 294; *Hist. Eccl.* i. l.c.

In matters of church discipline the legates paid no great heed to duty or decorum. When the unpopular Bishop of Hólar, Orm Asláksson, left his diocese for Norway in 1354, he had appointed as his vicar the abbot of Thingeyrar, a Benedictine monastery in the North,[21] by name Arngrím Jónsson. But in such disfavour was this man with the clergy of the diocese that they refused collectively to recognize his authority. A diocesan Synod suspended him, not only from his functions as bishop's vicar, but also from his office as abbot of Thingeyrar. Anticipating the disgrace likely to result from the decision of the Synod the wily abbot by a sudden shift threw off the Benedictine for the Dominican garb, as if he earnestly and indeed desired to renounce the world, pretending at the same time that he was minded to go abroad, in order to join a Dominican community at Bergen, as in Iceland the order had no house wherein to receive him. But when the legates made their appearance in the northern diocese they forthwith reinstalled Arngrim in his abbotship of Thingeyrar—at his own solicitation, no doubt—unreleased from his Dominican vows, an act which seems to have created great scandal in the church.[22]

Such was this Norwegian visitation, of which no further positive records are known. It was, as most official trans-

[21] This monastery owned its origin to a vow for a better season made by the Bishop of Hólar, Jón Ogmundsson, 1106–21, in the midst of a large congregation at a spring-mote, a short time after his promotion to that see. But contributions towards the establishment of a religious house at the place came in so slowly, that it was not fully established till 1133. Biskupa Sögur, Kaupmannahöfn, 1858, i. 171, *Annals*, 58, *Hist. Eccl.* iv. 29–30. It fell in 1551.

[22] *Hist. Eccl.* iv. 34; *Annals*, 294.

actions of the time, lawless in the extreme. The men in authority were a corrupt class, generally speaking. And from perusing the various annals relating to this period of Icelandic history, one gathers the impression that the unscrupulous career of public men was apt to terminate near to, when not on, the gallows, or under the fatal blows of an infuriated populace. The Icelandic suffragans of Drontheim were Norwegians, more intent upon doing the will of their Metropolitan master than promoting the weal of their flocks. Church and state went hand in hand, enriching themselves by the spoils of the people. In consequence, demoralisation and reckless disregard of the authority of the law reigned supreme through all classes of society. Under such circumstances, it was not to be wondered at, that these servants of alien interests should turn out rather disseminators of discord and scandal, than promoters of what lay far beyond their master's programme—peace and goodwill among men.

About this time it befell that Bishop Gyrd and Brother Eystein became bitter enemies. This strife took its rise, undoubtedly, from matters connected with Eystein's official position,[23] but the immediate causes of it are not known with the exception of some ludicrous stories which give it the tone of a discreditable personal squabble of a purely private nature. It would seem that the caustic friar had outwitted the Bishop, and pelted him, *ex improviso*, with impure and contemptuous rhymes, which it would serve no purpose to repeat, and had applied to his person such language as 'ball-bellied,' and other epithets of a still less ornamental character.[24] Bishop Gyrd, in all probability less

[23] This is hinted at in the *Annals*, Anno 1358, p. 292; *Espolin*, i. 88.

[24] *Hist. Eccl.* i. 587; *Espolin*, i. 88; *Biskupa Annálar Jóns Egilssonar* in Safn til Sögu Islands, Kaupmannahöfn, 1865, i. 33.

stout of heart than his assailant deemed he was of body, seems, according to Bishop Jónsson, to have given way at last to such unseemly display of temper as to afford to the insolent Brother a pretence for summoning him before the Metropolitan of the province. But the Bishop, recognising his position, answered the summons by the thunder of excommunication, just as both prepared to leave the country in 1358 for Norway.[25] This brought the haughty legate to his senses, and forced him to take an humiliating view of his forlorn condition. Contrition of heart wrought in him a wholesome change; he repented sincerely and obtained full absolution from the Bishop, who received him again into his favour, and good-naturedly enough appointed him his vicar for the western portion of his diocese, as he himself soon afterwards embarked for Norway (1359). The vessel wherein the Bishop sailed foundered some distance off the coast of Iceland, but all hands were saved in a miraculous manner through a vow to the holy Thorlak, and were landed by a small craft on the same shore they had left in the ill-fated vessel.[26]

The following year Bishop Gyrd and Brother Eystein left Iceland severally for Norway, never to return again. The vessel in which the Bishop sailed was wrecked on the Faroe Islands, and all hands were lost.[27] But Eystein tossed about the stormy Atlantic even into the heart of winter, and having sustained dreadful hardships, hunger, and thirst, was at last dashed upon the rocky shore of Helgoland in Norway, where he barely escaped with

[25] *Hist. Eccl.* i. 587, 588; *Espolin*, i. 88; *Annals*, 292, 294.
[26] *Hist. Eccl.* ii. 105; *Annals*, 296; *Espolin*, i. 89.
[27] *Hist. Eccl.* ii. 105; *Annals*, 298–300; *Espolin*, i. 92.

life from the wrecked vessel. Destitute of all he had in this world, and brought low with hard trials, he made for the home of Elgisetr, where he arrived about Candle-mass (Feb. 2) 1360. Now his life drew rapidly to its close; and he fell asleep towards the tide of Passio Domini, 1361.[28]

Such is our Brother's sad and short history. It is too fragmentary to justify any decided estimate of his moral character. The fragments of his life which we still possess exhibit certainly some features which we should like to present a more pleasing aspect; but then they are the mere recorded results—how far faithfully represented we are unable to tell—of the conflicting influences of surrounding temptations, which are almost entirely hidden from view, so that we know nothing as to how powerfully they may have operated on Eystein's mind, nor how stoutly he may have met them before he was defeated. As known to us he stands almost entirely disunited from the social life that made him; but indications are not wanting to show that that society was rotten to the very core. It is therefore not to be wondered at that it produced no healthy growth in an easy-living friar, strongly imbued with the vices inherent in the *genus irritabile vatum*, haughty, wanton and witty. He stood too high, besides, in the social scale to escape being carried away by the avalanche of corruption which at this time swept from both thrones, royal and archiepiscopal, into the lower strata of society, and left it a sad waste of vice and stormy passions. But whatsoever his short-comings may have been, he must have been endowed with many engaging qualities to

[28] *Annals*, 302.—Some *Annals* refer his death to 1366; *Hist. Eccl.* i. 588; *Espolin*, i. 92.

counterbalance them. He was a learned man, according to the statement of the *Annals*,[29] a poet of a high order for his time, and must have been gifted with many personal fascinations to be able to play so fast and loose with the feelings and dignity of Bishop Gyrd, and yet to come out of the hazardous play, not only unscathed, but even a bosom friend of the Bishop. As apt as he seems to have been to fall a victim to the impetuosity of his temper, as ready also does he appear to have been to see and acknowledge his faults, when the *bearserks-gang* of his passion wore off. The 'Lily,' too, bears a clear testimony that the fire of devotion was burning in the deep of his soul, that his faith was nurtured by prayer, that his sense of humility was profound and unfeigned, and that his yearning for that grace which alone can assuage the sufferings of a troubled and contrite heart was fervid and sincere.

The folk-lore of Iceland has preserved the following quaint and original tale of Eystein as a magic minstrel:—

Brother Eystein so roused Bishop Gyrd's wrath by puns and pert rhymes that the latter had him taken prisoner and thrown into a dark pit underground, a hundred feet deep. In this plight Eystein began to compose 'Lilja.' When he had finished twenty-two stanzas of the song, he discovered, in good sooth, that he was gradually being lifted up from his dungeon. And great was his astonishment when he found, by some means or other, that he was really twenty-two feet above the floor of the prison: the reason of this could be none other than a latent power in his song. An overwhelming sense of joy pervaded the aggrieved penitent, and in his

[29] *Annals*, 292.

inspiration—but, alas! mixed with unseemly pride—he broke out into the too selfish twenty-third stanza:

> 'All fiery grows my tongue, my word
> In graceful strain extols the Lord;
> Of his most wondrous works I sing
> Who doth embrace world's threefold ring.'

Scarcely had the last word died away on his lips, when down tumbled the bard all the twenty-two steps he had already risen, and lay prostrate on the floor of his dark pit. On recovering from the shock, he thought the lesson had been taught him well enough that 'pride goes before a fall,' and in the humblest of moods he now concluded the stanza:

> 'All bent I were 'neath ban and woe
> And bonds of that infernal foe,
> Had not my God's salvation free
> Been sent on earth to ransom me.'[30]

The sincere humility of this semi-strophe sufficed to send the afflicted sinner all the twenty-three steps up again, and henceforth his upward progress continued unbroken, one step for every finished stanza, until he had sung himself fairly out of prison.

Another legend knows that he not only got out of prison by the poem 'Lily,' but that he even sang Bishop Gyrd 'stone-dead.' He never made any hurtful use, however, of the magic power of his song but on the direst provocation and in defence of self, and slew none by it but one ponderous prelate.

[30] Here, of course, a different text is followed from that adopted in the poem itself.

II.

The Poem 'Lilja.'

1. TEXT.

The present text of 'Lilja' is based on two MSS. principally. One of these is found in the Royal Library in Stockholm, bearing the name of 'Bergs ábóta bók,' or 'Konungabók af Bergi ábóta,' a parchment in folio; No. 1 in the collection called 'Islandica.' My learned friend, Mr. Jón Sigurdsson of Copenhagen, has most kindly favoured me with the various readings of this MS., as compared with the last edition of 'Lilja,' Copenhagen, 1858. He takes the handwriting of 'Lilja' in this volume to be of the fifteenth century. The song has no title, but a note, in handwriting of the seventeenth century, in Danish, takes its place:—'Dette er itt merckeligt Rim och kaldis denn Lilliæ;' *i. e.* This is a remarkable rhyme, and is called Lilliæ. It takes up nearly seven pages in the MS., foll. 113^{b}–116. Of the orthography of this MS. Mr. Sigurdsson had given me a short account; but as I could not think of giving a phonetic representation of the text, I need not enter into that matter here. The text of this MS., called B in the notes, forms the basis of the present edition. This is the best text known of the song, and has not been edited before.[31]

The second MS., represented in the notes where its

[31] See Arwidson's 'Förteckning öfver kongl. Bibliothekets i Stockholm isländska handskrifter.' Stockholm, 1848.

reading is at variance with B's, but often also superseding the authority of B in the text, is found in the British Museum Library, Ayscough, 4892, small octavo, called A in the notes. It is one in that collection of Icelandic MSS. which Sir Joseph Banks presented to the British Museum after his visit to Iceland in 1772. Sir Joseph Banks, it appears, had given a commission to O. Stephensen, then governor of the south presidency of Iceland, and residing at Svedholt on Alptanes, to 'collect as many *antiquities*, and have copied as many histories, as could be found in the country.' The commission was readily undertaken by Stephensen; who, instead of complying with Sir Banks' stipulation of having the stories copied, bought up volume after volume as he found them, and shipped them to England in large lots. A first instalment left the country in 1773;[32] a second, consisting of 'eighteen stories,' was despatched in 1775;[33] and a third in 1777, consisting of 'thirty-five histories,' besides 'antiquities and annals.' This lot contained two, if not three, parchments, and the diligent governor points two of them out with particular pride: the first, the old code of the country, 'Jónsbók,' as being 'five hundred years old,' and, of course, 'the oldest copy to be had in the country;'[34] the second, a 'Papal hymn-book,' likewise 'very rare, interesting, and curious, on account of its contents.'[35] This is the

[32] Letter from O. Stephensen to Sir Joseph Banks, dated Svedholt, June 24, 1773. (Mus. Brit. Ex legato J. Banks, No. 8094, Plut. clxxi. fols. 34–35.)

[33] Letter from O. Stephensen to Sir Joseph Banks, dated Svedholt, August 25, 1775. (Ib. fols. 122–123.)

[34] It is a fourteenth-century MS. of Jónsbók, in excellent preservation. At the end it bears the name of Jón Jónsson (lawman 1573–1603?)

[35] Letter from O. Stephensen to Sir Joseph Banks, dated Svedholt, August 20, 1777. (Ib. fols. 256–257.)

last transmission from Stephensen that I can trace. Under the title of 'Catholsk Psalmebog,' this MS. figures in the British Museum Catalogue of the Banksian collection of Icelandic MSS. from 1782; but it bears now (rebound in 1868) the title of 'Hymns to the Virgin, &c.'

As the contents of this MS. are, to my knowledge, given nowhere else, I give them here, for the benefit of those who take an interest in the sacred poetry of the middle ages. I give of each song the commencing and the final line.

i. Latin: Fols. 1–5ᵃ, containing Invocations to the sign of the holy Cross, to God, to Jesus Christ, the Angels, the Apostles, the Holy Spirit, the Holy Trinity, the Blessed Virgin, the Saints, Patriarchs, Prophets, &c., followed by a fragment of the 85th Psalm, the doxology, Paternoster, and Prayers to the Virgin.

ii. Icelandic: Fols. 5ᵇ–60, containing,—

1. ✠ (*i e.* kross), Qviða

Hlýðið allir, ýtar snjallir, óði mínum.

* * * *

Þinn elskulegur sómi.—43 verses.

2. ✠ Qviða:

María, drottning, mild ok skær.

* * * *

Föður, Anda ok Syni sè súngin gloríá.—32 vv.

3. Maríu vísur:

Sancta María, móðir mild.

* * * *

Utan enda svá standi.—5 vv.

4. Maríu vísur:

María móðirin skæra, minning þín ok æra.

* * * *

Er móðir sönn at Eli.—6 vv.

5. Maríu vísur :

María, heyr mik, háleitt víf.

* * * *

Hlýð þú máli mínu.—8 vv.

6. Maríu vísur :

Dýrðarlegast dygða blóm.

* * * *

Servum pulsat mare.—2 vv.

7. Niculásar diktr :

Dýrðarfullur Drottinn minn.

* * * *

Blíður Niculás.—20 vv.

8. Sti. Olafs konungs diktr :

Herra Olaf, hjálpin Norðurlanda.

* * * *

Lof þitt jafnan súngit sè.—13 vv.

9. Ljómr Jóns Arasonar :

Hæstur Heilagur Andi

* * * *

Ætíð hefir mik þó til Drottins (defect).—23 vv.

10. Lilja (defect).

11. Agnesar kvæði (defect) :

. . . líta

Gull ok silfur nóglegt þá

* * * *

Sem helgust heiðrar Agnesá.—22 vv.

12. Barböru diktr :

Fyrir Distal rèði drengur heiðinn.

* * * *

Ætíð blessun lát oss fá, heilög meyjan Barbará.—26 vv.

13. Salutatio Mariæ :

Maria melli plena.

* * * *

Æ fyrir utan enda.—21 vv.

14. Maríu grátr:

Blómstrit brúða ok kvenna

* * * *

Allir segi, er á hafa hlýtt, Ave Maria.—17 vv.

15.

María Drottins liljan Guðs og ljómi.

* * * *

Ok brjósti þínu blessuð mær.—3 vv.

16. Maríu lykill:

Drottning œðsta, dýr af ættum.

* * * *

Lengi svá verði endir enginn.—61 vv.

17. Maríu vísur (defect, the wanting first thirteen verses may be supplied from Add. MS. 11,179):

. . . þeirra stræta
Þenna úrskurð heyrði upp á María.

* * * *

Mèr at hjálpa nauðum frá, María.—24 vv.

18. Maríu vísur gamlar:

Suptúngs vilda ek bjórinn blanda.

* * * *

Per omnia secula.—14 vv.

This MS. cannot lay claim to any higher antiquity than the latter half of the sixteenth century, which is evident from its containing many songs by Bishop Jón Arason, the last Pre-Reformation bishop of Iceland, beheaded 1550. On page 4 of the MS. there occur some figures inserted between the lines, which seem to represent the Runic letter ᛘ = M followed by 86 D. If any inference could be drawn from these figures with reference to the date of the MS. they would give the very probable date of 1586 (ᛘ = 1000 + D = 500 + 86). The MS is written throughout in one handwriting, with the exception of a portion of fol. 45; it is defective in three places, as the list of contents indicates. Every stanza of the 'Lily' is divided into two halves, each beginning with a Gothic initial, yellowish-red, blue, or green, without any fixed rule. Each burthen (stef) is marked by a trefoil before, and in the same colour as, its initial. The orthography is very inconsistent, apes ancient modes of spelling, accentuates vowels, and doubles consonants at random; in that point the MS. has no worth. The 'Lily' covers fols. 25–40.

Besides these two MSS. I have consulted the existing editions of the 'Lily.' The first, in 'Su gamla Vijsnabook, Hoolum, 1612,' I have not been able to get access to; but the edition of 1748, which purports to be an exact reprint of it, I have compared with the MSS., and followed in a couple of instances. Let me mention here that these editions of the 'Lily' are vicious, because Arngrim Jónsson, the learned, has presumed to alter the original wilfully, for the purpose of suiting it to bad Protestant tastes, wherever it struck him as being too redundant with the so-called Papistic leaven. The next edition is the one in Bishop Finn Jónsson's 'Hist. Eccl.' tom. ii. p. 399–447, accompanied by a Latin translation in prose by the Rev. Páll Hallsson, ob. 1663. This is a critical edition; and the bishop has collated many MSS., and attached to the text a good many various readings. The authority of this edition is followed in a few instances. A third edition, with a very Roman preface to it in French and Icelandic, and accompanied by a very close Latin translation, appeared, under Roman Catholic auspices, at Copenhagen, 1858; it is almost a close reprint of Finn Jónsson's text, and has, therefore, been of no aid to the text-critic of the present edition. A reprint of the Latin translation of this edition appeared at Vienna, 1859. A metrical translation of the 'Lily,' in Latin, by Páll Hallsson, is printed in 'Hist. Eccl.' ii. 448–64.

It may be safely stated that all previous editions of this song have left its text unintelligible in numbers of instances, as any one who may care to take the trouble of inquiring into the subject may soon see for himself. In the present edition these deficiencies are reduced to, at least, a small number; indeed the text may be said now to be intelligible throughout, although a few passages still defy good grammar.[36] I have left them as I found them, both because no serious doubt can be entertained as to the sense of the context, and because I do not see my way, after several attempts, to a conjectural restitution equally satisfactory to the exigencies of the context and of good grammar.

To technicalities of rhyme and metre greater attention is paid in the present than in any previous edition. In that point I was once about adopting a systematic restoration, on the strict principle of Eddaic precepts; but I gave it up because it seemed, and seems still to me, doubtful how far the poet has considered himself bound by the strict metric rules of the Edda, ignoring as he does its rules for allegorical and circumlocutory poetry. The liberal use of intercalarious short syllables throughout the song is, moreover, not an accident of oral tradition, or of a scribe's looseness: it is evidently, in the main, a genuine feature of Eystein's poetry.

I have not adopted a strict system of orthography in minor matters; thus the terminations *ið* and *að* interchange with *it* and *at;* and in different small matters of

[36] These places are especially stanzas 12, 7-8; 22, 1-2; 30, 2; 45, 5-6.

this kind I have chosen to be guided by sense of euphony, rather than by any rigidly carried out principle. In one particular my orthography differs from the usual standard; I have written *f*, but not *p*, before a *t*, where origin and kindred languages favour such orthography. In this I follow the very worthy authority of my friend, Mr. Jón Thorkelsson, Senior Master of Reykjavík College, one of the most learned of Northern philologists, and certainly one of the soundest Icelandic scholars living.[37]

---

2. METRICAL CONSTRUCTION.

In point of form, though not of argument, the 'Lily' belongs to that kind of Northern song known as the 'drápa.' This word, which is a derivative, and not a primitive one, is variously explained. Its root is clearly to be traced to the strong transitive verb drepa (Goth. *ga-draban*, Old Engl. *drepan*, Germ. *treffen*, North Engl. *drop*, East Engl. *drepe*, Dan. *dræbe*, Swed. *dräpa*), *to knock, strike, beat, smite, slay; to cram together*. From this last sense an explanation has been launched of drápa, as being a song cramful of praises; but we may dismiss it at once as a meagre philological vagary. Another explanation of the word has been attempted on the basis of an association of ideas suggested by the Greek δράω, *facio*, with the Northern verki, *work*, *poema*, and yrkja, *to work*, spec. *carmen facere*, resulting in the conclusion that drápa was

[37] Author of several most valuable critical essays on Icelandic literature, history, and philology, and editor of that portion of Hauksbók which in Cleasby's Icelandic-English Dictionary is cited as an edition of 1865.

κατ' ἐξόχην, *præstantissimum quodque poëmatis genus:* another vagary scarcely more to the purpose than the first. A third explanation, more to the point, at all events, than either of these, starts from the verb drepa in the sense of smiting a strung instrument; consequently the sense of drápa is given as *a song* in general (Cleasby, *sub voce* 'Drepa,' A 1), or 'an heroic, laudatory poem,' accompanied by music (*see* 'Drápa' in Cleasby). This stands to reason, of course; but I have in vain searched for an instance of a drápa ever having been delivered to the accompaniment of music. It is not to be forgotten that drápa is no general term to begin with; its etymology points to a song, unto which a name was given derived from external accessories, but not from its internal and elementary qualities. Now if it drew its name from the act of smiting the strings of a musical instrument, we may be sure that such a favourite occupation could not have been exercised among any people for any length of time without their giving some name to an act which thrilled them with delight, and kindled in their breasts the fire of enthusiasm. This act, which we name 'play,' the Germans 'spiel,' the Danes 'spil,' the Swedes 'spel,' is not to be found in Icelandic in any radical connexion with the verb drepa. We have two neuter derivatives of it, dráp and drep, but neither of these happens to occur in any musical sense whatever: both refer exclusively to the fundamental notion of smiting, killing; the first meaning manslaughter, the second a blow (in the juridical sense of bodily injury), manslaughter; destruction of life, either by the elements of nature or by plague, as the case may be. In this derivation of *drápa* we have therefore to encounter the difficulty how, by any natural process of the human thought, a distinct name can be given to the result of an action without that action having first got its own name, when there can be no question at all that the result must have derived its name from the very term given to the action which produced it. There could have been no difficulty in the way of giving a fitting name, even one derived from drepa, to the action in question—greater difficulties are got over in the formation of words in primitive times, for language, we know, is a very fruitful field in the spring-tide of human civilisation, when man's swift thought, quickened and inspired by his experiences, begins in earnest to work its virgin soil; and as regards music, this remark, I conceive, is applicable with all the force its words convey. I cannot but consider this third interpretation of drápa as suspicious, at all events. A fourth proceeds from drepa, in the sense of killing: '*quando quidem poemata laudativa olim non minimam partem circa pugnas et strages describendas versabantur*,' and seems to me to be the one which bears inspection. Etymologically I prefer connecting it with dráp, *the act of slaying, slaughter*, and venture to render it *slaughter-lay*, or *the lay of the slain*. Drápa is evidently a younger word than dráp, in proof of which is its termination, if it is indeed to be taken as a direct derivative of dráp.[38] And however that

[38] It is a curious fact that the organic relation of drápa to its verb finds, as I believe, scarcely another exactly congruous example in the Icelandic language. If we examine the nouns derived from the strong verbs belonging to the same class as drepa, we shall find that not one case affords an exact parallel to drápa: gefa, *to give*, generates gáfa, *gift;* geta, *to guess*, gáta, *a guess, a riddle;* þyggja, *to accept*, þága, *acceptance*. These are the nearest examples I can find. Their signification as well as the form is a natural outgrowth of the verb, whereas drápa in that respect is disunited from its parent stock, and can be connected with it only by the link of the neuter dráp. Can we suppose that

may be, so much seems certain, that originally a drápa was a song of the slain: it was a record of battles and warfare, commemorating, in poetical form—the securest preservative of unwritten history—for coming generations the memories of the exploits of their forefathers. The leaders of the combating hosts were, of course, the centres, round whom the praise of the drápa eddied. By the very nature of things the drápa could only be a song of praise, as antiquity was neither civilised enough to relish the delight of trampling upon a dead man's dust, nor wooden-headed enough not to understand that the praise of the surviving victor rested entirely upon the higher or lesser valour of his vanquished antagonist. By lapse of time the term drápa got a wider sense, and was applied to any song of praise; and finally the form, rather than the contents, decided whether a song was properly a drápa or not. The main distinguishing features of a drápa are length, metre, and burthen. It seems that a shorter poem than twenty stanzas came within the category of flokkr, or dræplingr; but one above twenty stanzas within that of the drápa. The 'drapas' themselves vary in the number of their stanzas from twenty up

drápa may be in a similar case with the names of those Icelandic sagas which in conventional usage have dropped the noun saga, leaving the genitive plural shorn to form a regular feminine? Examples, as Sturlúnga saga Sturlanorum historia, Eyrbyggja saga Eyranorum historia, Reykdœla saga Reykdalensium historia, have, by dropping saga, turned the masculine genitive plural into regular feminines. Is it likely that drápa can be a genitive plural from dráp, the feminine kviða, *a lay*, having been dropped; and that drápa-kviða, *slaughter-song*, was the original construction? The parallel between such formation and the above-mentioned examples is not exact in this one point, that the former proceed from a masculine, the drápa from a neuter. I leave the suggestion for scholars more competent than I am to settle.

to one hundred; they need not necessarily contain a stef or burthen, but as a rule they do, and by virtue of that characteristic are called stefja-drápur (burthen-lays). The metre is commonly, though by no means exclusively, the so-called drótt-kvæðr háttr. This term is of uncertain meaning, drótt signifying both the number *twenty* and the *body-guard* of a king; kvæðr, a verbal adjective from kveða, meaning *to be sung:* it may therefore mean either a metre to be used for songs sung in twenties, in twenty stanzas, or for songs to be delivered to a king and his men.

A perfect stefjadrápa must consist of introduction, burthen-lay, and finale (inngangr, stefjamál, slæmr), introduction + finale making up a number of stanzas equal to that of the burthen-lay. These formalities are strictly observed in 'Lilja,' which falls into the following portions:—

1. Inngangr, introduction; twenty-five stanzas.
2. Stefjamál (stave-lay?), burthen song; fifty stanzas.
3. Slæmr, finale; twenty-five stanzas.

The stefjamál of 'Lilja' fall into two portions, each divided from the other, and from the rest of the poem, by a special burthen, five times repeated in either at the regular interval of five stanzas. The skeleton of the song may be thus represented:—

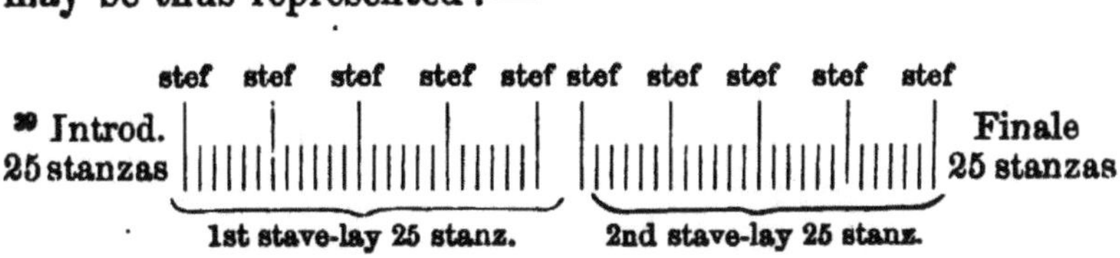

[39] It would have given a clearer survey of the poem if I had given the technical titles to the various portions of the poem in the text itself, and called the two stefjamál by one comprehensive title, stefja-bálkr, stave lot, and had numbered the staves.

The word stef means the strophe, in the case of 'Lilja' the half strophe, which cuts the introduction and the finale from the main body of the song—the stefjamál. It probably never meant but *bar*, as does, indeed, the English word *stave*, which I have chosen in the translation to represent it; for it *bars* or *staves off* from the *stave-lay* those portions of the song which do not belong to it. The artificial repetition of it within the stave-lay itself is purely optional. Although I have occasionally rendered stef as burthen, merely for the purpose of making myself understood, it has in its origin and application nothing beyond a superficial semblance in common with a burthen or refrain of a song, in the foreign acceptation of these terms.

The metre of 'Lilja' comes, as I have said before (p. xxxiii), within the range of the dróttkvæðr háttr, and represents that of its many variations, which is known as the dróttkvæða hrynjandi—the precipitating, dropping, or running sort of dróttkvæðr háttr. The special characteristic of that variation is, that each line must needs consist of eight syllables. The measure of it is purely trochaic; and it is not uninteresting to see how the same metric quality has struck the sense of the Greek and the Scandinavian in exactly the same manner, leading in either case, the one entirely independent of the other, to a descriptive term for it in reality identical. The author of 'Lilja' has not bound himself by any rigorous adherence to the law of his chosen metre, but has tampered with its detail in various ways, being content with adhering to the principle of it in its vague generality. I doubt, however, that he was conscious of the license he allowed himself in this respect. It is pretty clear that in Eystein's time the poets were beginning to treat the accent of the language in a much looser way than the poets of the thirteenth, not to speak of those of earlier centuries. The reason of it is obvious. When the Christian literature began to engross the mind of the poets, the Eddaic rules seem to have clashed with their sense of propriety, as unsuitable for conveying reverentially enough the devotional character of a sacred song. The essential nature of that kind of song being simplicity and pellucidity conveyed in words from the heart, and appealing to the heart, all the old artificiality, the object of which was to conceal the real meaning, and make every poetical effort a piece of puzzling brain-work, could be turned to account no longer. The old poetry, besides, was, no doubt, beginning to be imperfectly understood by this time, and the old prosodic laws to be forgotten. When the authority of Eddaic rules, the old metrical laws, began thus to be disregarded, a new era in Icelandic poetry was inaugurated, marked by simplicity of diction, a loose and jolting rhythm, and a vague regard to the accent. Compared with the old poetry in this respect, the fourteenth-century poetry appears as a dim recollection of a thing once well known and clearly understood. Let it, however, be borne in mind that these observations apply, as far as the 'Lily' is concerned, to detail, not to general principles.

Let us now examine the general law of the metre of 'Lilja'—a law which applies in great measure to all Icelandic metres. We need only take a couplet or two in order to explain the whole. Let us take, by way of example, the two first couplets of the opening stanza:—

> **A**lmáttigr Guð **a**llrar stèttar,
> **Y**fir-bjóðandinn engla ok þjóða,
> Ei þurfandi **st**aða nè **st**unda,
> **St**að haldandi í kyrrleiks valdi.

The first thing to be observed is the regularity wherewith the two lines in either couplet are linked together, as it were, with more or less identical characters; two in the first line, at measured intervals, which may never stand so far apart as that the phonetic *rapport* in which they stand to one another be weakened or destroyed; and one at the head of the second line, höfuðstafr, *head-letter*, which by way of license may sometimes be preceded by a short syllable. In the couplets before us these letters are **a a | y** in the first, **st st | st** in the second. These letters bear suggestive names in Icelandic prosody. The two of the first line are called stuðlar, *i.e. props*, *stayers*, or *pillars*, because they give stay and stability, as it were, to the metre; as is evident when a poet, having composed the first line of the couplet, is bound by that line not to use whatso word he chooses to begin the next, but such word only of which the commencing letter or letters harmonise identically with the stuðlar. The function of the *head-letter* is, therefore, to bring the second line in each couplet into an alliterative harmony with the first line. If the stuðlar and höfuðstafr are consonants, no matter whether single or double, it is entirely unlawful that any other word in the couplet should begin with the same letter (or letters); if they are vowels (diphthongs), one monosyllable, short, and beginning with a vowel, may be introduced in the proper place: such, however, is license, not law. Hence, *e*ngla, following *y*fir-bjóðandinn, in the first couplet of 'Lilja,' is against the law of the metre. This alliterative law being thus strictly laid down and observed, even in the very earliest monuments of Northern song, shows how early Northern bards, with their keen sense for euphony, and with remarkably good taste, set their faces against excessive alliteration and redundant assonance. This law of alliteration obtains throughout all Icelandic poetry, and rules equally supreme in the stateliest drápa and the commonest ditty.

But there is a special law, regulating the metre of 'Lilja' as a variation of the dróttkvæðr háttr, which we have still to make ourselves acquainted with—the law of assonance. Taking the first couplet of 'Lilja,' which may well serve as *instar omnium*, whereas the whole poem is but a succession of couplets, ruled by one and the same unbroken law,—

Almáttigr Guð allra stétta
Yfir-bjóðandinn engla ok þjóða,

we see there are two syllables in each line, at measured intervals, which, phonetically speaking, stand, in the first line, in a non-unisonous, in the second, in a fully unisonous *rapport* to one another. These syllables are called hendingar, which, for want of a better word,—as *catch* or *catches* would be deemed too daring, I fear—I am obliged to call *rhyme syllables.* Those of the first line are called skot-hendingar, an untranslatable term, implying that the latter rhyme syllable shoots from the first in such a manner as only 'to take after it' as it were, or vaguely to resemble it. But those of the second line are called aðalhendingar, or identical rhyme syllables. Each of these syllables, taken separately, is a hending; and the first bears the name of frumhending, or first hending, which, according to its place in the verse, is called oddhending if it commences the line, but hluthending—hlut from hluta, *to divide in twain*—if it stands in the middle of it, as Snorri lays down the rule; but, more accurately speaking, occupies in it the place of the third syllable which is invariably long. The latter rhyme syllable bears the name of viðrhending, implying that it stands as a pendant or counterpoise to the first hending. This rhyme syllable precedes invariably the last syllable in each verse. The hendingar must terminate in the same consonant or consonants, as also the couplet before us teaches us: má*tt*—stè*tt*, bjóð—þjóð; but they may begin in whatso way one pleases, as long as they do not exceed the restrictive rules for alliteration and assonance. It is entirely unlawful that a third syllable, phonetically identical with either of the rhyme syllables, should stand in the same line. It is desirable that the skothending should represent a vowel sound belonging to the same class of vowels as that of its prototype, the frumhending; that is to say, a skothending should represent an open and closed vowel sound, according as the case is with the frumhending—as f. e. Ei þurf*a*ndi staða nè st*u*nda; Hjörtun j*á*ti fagni ok flj*ó*ti, &c. But this rule, although generally observed, is frequently disregarded in 'Lilja.' It enhances the beauty of, and gives greater rhythmical weight to, this kind of dróttkvæðr háttr when the frumhending occupies the place of the hluthending, *i.e.* at ⏑ – ⏑ in front of the viðrhending, for in that case the natural weight of the rhythm coincides with the phonetic centre of gravity of the line, f. e. þrætug*járn* með klókar *varn*ir; skepnan *öll* er skyld at *fall*a, &c. A mere instinctive observance of this rule is traceable in 'Lilja,' but it does not seem to be carried out on any settled principle. The law of assonance, of which I have thus endeavoured to give a sketch, both in its generality and in its more palpable detail, rules with great amount of precision throughout the 'Lilja,' and is very carefully observed; and it is not to be considered as an infringement of it that vowels, which can apparently only form skothendíngar, y and i, ý and í, œ and æ, do form aðalhendíngar, for in Eystein's lifetime they had become identical. The only case where Eystein has made a slip in this respect is 68, 8, where ý and y are made to form an aðalhending. Let me mention, finally, that the skothendingar must of necessity occupy a place in the first line, and can never interchange their position in a couplet with that of the aðalhendíngar.

In the preceding exposition of the metric construction of 'Lilja' I have had to deal with some curious technical terms of the prosody, of genuine Scandinavian origin, which we have not yet considered in their derivative aspect. I have already had occasion to advert to the practical application of stuðlar and the höfuðstafr, and I have shown that their names indicate the firm stability or settled turn which they give to the metre. Now stuðull means originally *a pillar-stone, basaltic pillar*, a formation frequently found in the North; hence stuðla-berg, *sheer basaltic pillar-rocks;* Stuðlar, a name given to farmsteads situate in close vicinity of such rocks. Again, stafr means exactly the same thing originally, as the very old local names of Stafa-holt, Stafa-fell, Stafa-ey = Staffa, so clearly indicate. Both these words, which thus originally were appellatives of natural objects, were borrowed for the prosodic terminology, when man began to be conscious of his poetry as being art, and the laws of it revealed themselves to his awakened thought, in the plastic reality of the surrounding rocks in nature. The Runic, or oldest Northern alphabet,[40] consisted of mere

[40] Why do Englishmen use this Greek word, which none but the learned understand, when they have, or can have, a genuine term in their own language for it, quite as good and much more expressive: stave-row (= row of letters); old Engl. stæf-rawa?

pillars or staves, hence the appropriate transfer of the word stafr from a pillar-rock to what bore a striking resemblance to it, whether cut on stone or written on paper. The choice of stuðull as a descriptive term for that peculiar characteristic of Northern song which gave the impression of a rock-fast form, and by the means of which it became fixed in the memory in a manner reminding of the unshaken stability of the rock—and let it not be forgotten that the faithful preservation of olden poetry is, in a very large measure, due to these very stuðlar—seems a most appropriate one. We see now that there can be little doubt about the surrounding nature having served to furnish technical terms to the most palpable and striking qualities of Northern song, in the same manner as the tent with its appurtenances has supplied the nomadic Arab with his prosodical nomenclature.

But the hending? The word has never been explained, to my knowledge, except in its applicative phase. Etymologically it is to be derived from henda, a weak transitive verb meaning *to throw* (*to hand*), and to catch that which is thrown. Hence hending might seem to imply both modes of action. Here we have a word the fundamental notion of which is **action**, which is the salient point in the inquiry. We have therefore to search in the sphere of life for such a manifestation to which the impression of the metric assonance seemed to bear an especially suggestive resemblance. We may be certain that many a ringing song had struck upon the Northern ear before the listeners or the reciters, or the poets themselves, knew the name hending as a technical term for its assonance. This term was borrowed for the prosody when the act of hending was a *general* and *favourite* occupation, was loved and admired. And such a favourite this very action happens to be in a warlike race, when spear-throwing and other kinds of throwing have come to constitute the education of able-bodied citizens in the state. It is, therefore, by no means unlikely that the spear, hurled from the hand, and flying in a curved line through the air, hitting, or being caught by, the object aimed at, was found to bear such a striking resemblance to the sound of the frumhending, issued and travelling over the measured space of intervening syllables, and dashing against the consonantal wall, which, as it were, stopped it in its flight and prevented its travelling further, as to render natural and irresistible the transfer of the term of the real action over unto the supposed phonetic one. The action of throwing the spear, as well as that of catching it, is undoubtedly hending (henda spjót á lofti, *to catch a spear in the air*, is a standing military phrase of old), and the resemblance between these two parallels seems to me to stand to reason, at all events; although I do not presume at all to arrogate any infallibility for my view. Another suggestion lies also near in this matter. The verb henda in the phrase 'at henda spor' means *to make or take a step*, and is applied specially to the jerky, staggering beginning of a child's walk. If the word was of old used in this sense, of which I am not quite certain, however, the hending would be = pace or step, and would approach somewhat the Greek notion of foot-measure.

It is furthermore worth while noticing, that both the alliteration and the assonance of ancient Northern metres bear a striking resemblance to a reverberated echo. The echo itself, so frequent in basalt formations, in gulfs and gorges and mountain-rifts and valleys, bears in Icelandic the name of dverga-mál, *dwarf-speech*, and dwarfs inhabit sheer-rocks only. Anciently the dwarfs are closely connected with poetry. They were once upon a time the sole guardians of the art; for a while, at least, after the time when Fjalarr and Galarr had slain Kvasir, the incarnate Poetry, whose blood they preserved, mixed with honey, in the famous vats of Són and Boðn, and the kettle Oðrerir, or Oðreyrir. It is deeply interesting to see how the poetry of the people—whose mythic traditions ascribe the gift of it to a drink from the dwarf-guarded vats—should bear in its phonetic fall an audible evidence of the antiquity of those traditions.

Let me finally mention a τεχνοπαίγνιον, of which Eystein has made use in this poem, occurring in stanzas 49 and 55, and consisting in a repetition at the commencement of each successive line of the same word in which the preceding one terminates. Rhyme-plays of various kinds, indeed of an infinity of variation, are found diffused through all the artificial poetry of Iceland. That subject is far too wide for me to enter upon now. My attempt at giving a close representation of these stanzas in the translation has partially failed in the first instance: in the second I had to give it up altogether.

---

3. SOURCES.

It has always been supposed that the 'Lily' was a thoroughly original Icelandic production; but the notion will hold good neither as regards its framework nor yet as the subject-matter is concerned. The frame is borrowed partly from the general outline of the much-admired hexaemerons, partly from Beda's detailed account of the contents of the songs of Cædmon, as may be seen from the foot-note to stanza 5, page 6. In the stanza cited, the enumeration of the topics of 'Lilja' are not an exact translation of Beda by any means; nor does it represent faithfully the general outlines of the contents of the 'Lily' itself, such as they actually are: but this is not to be wondered at when regard is had to the trammels of the rhyme, the vague notion the poet must have had at that stage of his song of what topics he might embody in it, and the narrow space he allowed himself for the enumeration of the various heads of his argument. The themes of the 'Lily' follow in their succession exactly the system of Cædmon, as Beda gives it, except in the matter of the Old Testament, which Eystein skips after the fall of man, and in the praises to the Virgin, wherein the Anglo-Saxon bard could not, of course, have been the Icelander's guide, for Cædmon lived too early to have known the Virgin in her deified glory. This at first seemed to point to a relationship between Cædmon and Eystein as that of master and pupil. I therefore examined and compared the two poets, but I found that, although great similarities existed between both, they were not greater than one might expect them to be naturally in two poems of epic character treating the same historic subject. Moreover, I looked in vain for any reminiscence in Eystein of certain *naïve* expressions of Cædmon's, which, on account of their peculiarly Eddaic tone, must have come home to an Icelandic poet with considerable force. Now although it may be possible that Eystein knew Anglo-Saxon,[41] and that he was conversant with Cædmon's poems, it is not to be proved from

[41] In the fourteenth century mention is frequently made of Anglo-Saxon books belonging to church and monastic libraries. See Jón Sigurdsson's learned observations on this point in the preface to 'Osvalds saga hins helga, the Saga of St. Oswald,' in Annaler for Nordisk Oldkyndighed, 1854, p. 17, note.

internal, and much less from external, evidence, that the songs of the latter served as a fountain for the 'Lily.' But Eystein's treatment of the history of the creation and the fall of man seems to point rather to Anglo-Saxon sources than to any ancient hexaemeron that I have seen. The story of the creation assumed very early in the Anglo-Saxon Church a stereotyped form, and occurs over and over again in Anglo-Saxon writers with slight variations. It is best told, perhaps, by Archbishop Ælfric in his homily on the creation, which agrees vaguely with the 'Veraldar Saga, Sex Etates Mundi,' in Professor Konrad Gíslason's edition in 'Pröver, Kjöbenhavn, 1860.' The Anglo-Saxon Church tradition differed from the Catholic in this essential point, that a stress is invariably laid on the number of the angels, as being ten instead of nine. The Anglo-Saxon tradition as Cædmon, and, in fact, the whole Anglo-Saxon Church knew it, is maintained by some scholars (Bouterwek and Gözinger, for instance) to have been derived from the teachings of Gregory the Great on the subject. But nothing that he has taught seems to give fair ground for this asseveration, except it be a remark in his thirty-fourth homily (on Luke, xv. 8–9), where, in explaining the mystic significance of the parable of the woman who lost one of her ten pence, he says, '*Sed ut compleretur electorum numerus homo decimus creatus est.*' But although Eystein follows the Catholic tradition in the number of the angel orders, he does seem to treat the whole hexaemeric subject exactly as the Anglo-Saxon tradition does: Beda's hexaemeron does not seem to have formed a model for him at all. Closely as he has followed the hexaemeric thread of the narrative of the creation, as it was known to the Anglo-Saxon Church, the wording of his verse seems to have been mostly influenced by that of the 'Elucidarium' of Honorius Augustodunensis.[42] This famous work on mediæval dogmatics was translated very early into Icelandic, and still exists in a fragmentary condition in a MS. of the latter end of the twelfth century, preserved in the Arnamagnæan collection at Copenhagen. Passages from the writings of the fathers of the Latin Church are reflected in the song here and there, and a few references of them are given in the foot-notes. The liturgy of the Church has greatly influenced the wording of the poem; but I have not given many citations from that source, because in the plurality of cases they seemed to be of a secondary importance.

4. TIME OF COMPOSITION.

On this point nothing can be said with certainty. The legendary notion is that the 'Lily' was composed in consequence of Bishop Gyrd having thrown Brother Eystein into prison; but legend alone knows of such imprisonment. He was incarcerated, in 1343, by Bishop Sigurdsson (p. ix), and was excommunicated by Bishop Gyrd in 1358. The two facts have been fused into one by the oral tradition of subsequent times, when the belief in magic and miracles, especially in the thaumaturgical powers of great poets, had come into vogue. There is something plausible in the idea that the composition of the song

[42] This theologian, surnamed Solitarius or Inclusus, is said to derive his name, Augustodunensis, either from Autun in Burgundy, or from Augst near Basel, where he is supposed to have been a teacher in the episcopal school. He died between 1130 and 1143. The Icelandic is the earliest known translation of this work.

might have been imposed upon Eystein, in expiation of some guilt which drew upon him severe censure from the Church. In that case we should expect the song to bear some internal testimony of such an origin: but no indication to that effect is to be gathered from any word in it; and even if that were the case it would not necessarily—unless it were specially stated—fix its time of composition to the period which followed upon his quarrel with Bishop Gyrd. However, the Annals state expressly that he composed the poem *after* he had libelled Bishop Gyrd[42]—which statement, if it is not a later interpolation, would be of great weight in the matter of this inquiry. But there are various considerations which seem to make this record suspicious. If the song had been composed in 1359, I cannot help thinking it must have exhibited more marks of hurry than it does. It gives one the impression of being the result of labour and care. This is especially the case with the stave-lay, where the balanced distribution of the themes of the song between the different staves is evidently the work of studied consideration. The various passages drawn from external sources may be reminiscences introduced *stante pede*, but they are quite as likely to be the result of research and study, which it is hard to reconcile with the hurried execution of imposed penalty. This year he was, besides, too much occupied with official duties to have found leisure enough for such an elaborate production as the 'Lilja' is. I am inclined to think that it dates from an earlier period of his life; perhaps from the time subsequent to his release from prison in 1343; and that his election in 1349 to be official of the diocese may have been in part due to the fame he had won for himself by the poem.

[42] *Annals*, 262.

5. POSITION IN ICELANDIC LITERATURE.

Our song belongs to a time when the so-called classical literature of Iceland had had its day, and the Church had taken possession of the field. Saga-writing had yielded the palm to the chronicler of contemporaneous events. The heroic poetry had receded into the quiet of the past, and the saint had taken the place in the popular mind of the dethroned Æsir. From the dash of the heroic *tempo di marzia* of the palmy days of war and viking-fare, Poetry had settled down into a tranquil twilight mood, brooding over a half-unconscious erotic sentiment, giving vent to it through pathetic balladry in a plaintive minor. The root of it was a religious sentiment, which, on the other hand, gave birth to a very bulky literature of Saint-lays, often full of sombre pathos, but very commonly teeming with an excessively turgid realism. Among the saints there was none to whose adoration so many songs sounded as the Virgin. She was the centre round which the sentimental contemplation of the age clustered. She was the sinner's last consolation—equally great in her power as in her love for man. She was the ideal of womanly virtue and purity, and was always imagined clothed in a transcendentally beauteous virginal form: as such only she could be understood by the realistic fourteenth-century world. The many poets who had sung her praise before this time were eclipsed by Eystein, not so much by his praises of her—although these may well be considered on a level with those of the famous Litany of Loretto—as by the superiority of his poetry and diction, and the large range of the poem in which the praise was embodied. If I am not mistaken, it is the only saint-lay in dróttkvæðr háttr of national origin which reaches the length of eight hundred lines. It is the most perfect stefja drápa of its kind known, and is couched in language equally sonorous and realistic. It therefore became at once the favourite of all classes. It sounded deliciously when recited, and it was easily learnt by heart, by reason of the enthusiasm its recitals created. Throughout the whole land it was soon known, and in such veneration was it held that, according to Finn Jónsson, some people deemed it a necessity to recite it in a loud voice daily, or once a-week at least; omitting this was considered a sign of impiety. Its recital was held almost tantamount to a public confession of faith. It has lived, by oral tradition principally, even to this day; and is, in the most out-of-the-way places in Iceland, still recited in a fragmentary condition. It is, on the whole, the greatest saint-lay of Iceland from the pre-reformation time; and not of Iceland alone, but of the whole of Scandinavia, according to the testimony of all scholars and historians who have touched upon the subject.

6. THE TRANSLATION.

My principle has been as close an adherence to the original as possible. I have tried to be literal, but have to confess that I have frequently failed. The original is not inviting for a treatment of that nature, nor have I that command of the English language which alone could secure success to such an undertaking. I hope, however, that I have succeeded in not misrepresenting the sense of my original in any marked degree. In cases where the wording is obscure, opinions will necessarily be divided as to how far I may have succeeded in eliciting the true sense. Crude expressions I have refrained from softening down—they belong to the time they date from, and have the same right to be faithfully represented as the rest. The chief beauty of the original—its stately and sonorous flow—I have utterly failed in reproducing in the translation. But it is not entirely due to individual shortcomings on my part. It is principally due to the language into which the translation is made. The thing cannot be done in English. Alliteration and assonance—the *raison d'être* of Icelandic poetry—are qualities which give it a tone, the reproduction of which it would be futile to essay in English, to which language neither characteristic belongs except by accident. However meagre the sense of Icelandic verse may be, if it is clothed in perfect form its inanity is overlooked and the outer beauty delighted in. Hence it is that Icelandic poetry generally addresses itself to the ear rather than to the thought—never, however, with an intentional disregard of the latter. In reading good Icelandic poetry we are frequently struck by the sound flashing, as it were, with illuminating effect across the cluster of ideas implied in the words, so as to fuse tone and thought and word into one inexpressibly harmonious and lucid reality. This characteristic, which depends to a large extent on the reciprocal reflex of alliteration and assonance, is met with nigh scores of times in 'Lilja,' and can be realised only by him who knows how to read it correctly. It belongs to things which are felt only, but cannot be explained, and no English translation can give the faintest notion of what it is like.

7. THE GLOSSARY

I have given very full, perhaps unnecessarily so. But I trust its fulness will be found rather an advantage than a source of complaint. I have not been content with giving such sense only of the words as they are found to convey in the text, but have frequently given a general survey of the scope of their meaning. As to the rest, I have only to explain a few technicalities in it.

In order to give a notion of the declension, the forms of the three cases, nom. and gen. sing., and nom. pl., are given throughout, the latter two within brackets immediately following the nom. sing.; an id. within these brackets signifies that the form which it replaces is identical with nom. sing.; a- prefixed to the termination within the brackets, stands for the root of the substantive—in case of neuters terminating in *i* it stands for nom. without the *i*; a– signifies that the form which it stands for does not occur, or is very rare.

Of all strong verbs occurring in the poem the following sign-forms are given: infinitive, 1 sing. pres. ind., 1 sing. and 1 pl. imp. ind., 1 sing. imp. subj., and the supine. Of the weak verbs are given the sign-forms 1 sing. imp. ind., and the past participle.

---

8. ARGUMENT.

I have shown above (page xxxiii), that the 'Lilja' falls technically into three main portions. The division of the argument corresponds with the technical division. This will be seen best by giving a schematic survey of the contents.

i. Introduction.—*The old covenant until the fall of man*, 1–26.—Invocation to God, 1–2; to the Virgin, 3; reasons for undertaking the work, 4; the themes of the song, 5; creation of the world and the angels, 6; fall of the latter, 7–9; the time it took to create the world, 10; creation of man, 11–13; God's command to the first parents, 15–17; fall of man, 18; the curse, 19; the spread of sin, 20; how is the world to be saved? 21; by a new life given to it, 22; address to his own tongue, 23; the work of salvation resolved upon in heaven, 24; praise to Mary, 25; doxology, 26.

ii. Stave-lay.—*The work of salvation*, 27–74.

First Stave-lay.—The Period from the Annunciation to the Crucifixion, 27–50.—The Annunciation, 27–31; the birth of Christ, 33–35; the three wise men from the East, 36; the baptism of Christ, 37; the devil's counsel, 38–43; the temptation, 45; miracles, 46; Judas' betrayal, 47–48; the crucifixion, 49.

Second Stave-lay.—The death of Jesus, to the triumph of the Church in heaven, 51–74.—Christ on the cross, 52; Mary's sorrow, 53–56; death of Jesus, 58; the wonders at His death, 59; the devil searches for sin on the cross, 60; descension to, and conquest of, hell, 61–62; reflections on the first and second Adam, 64; the devil censured, 65–66; resurrection and ascension into heaven, 67; the sending of the Holy Ghost, 68; the last judgment, 70; its justice, 71; division of good and evil, 72; tortures of hell, 73; joys of heaven, 74.

iii. Finale.—Prayers to God and Christ, 75-85; prayers to Mary, 86–95; dedication of the work, 96; address to the reader, 97; reasons why Eddaic rules are not heeded, 98; exhortation to recite the poem to Mary, together with her verse, *i. e.* 'Ave Maria,' 99.

SHORT GUIDE TO THE PRONUNCIATION OF THE ICELANDIC LETTERS.

VOWELS AND DIPHTHONGS.

Open: a, e, è, i, o, u, y, ö.
Closed: á, í, ó, ú, ý, æ, œ, au, ey, ei.

a sounds likes Italian *a*, and comes near to the English *a* followed by *sk* and *st*, as in task, fast.

á like *ow* in now or *ou* in stout.

au answers to no sound in the English language. It comes very near to the French *œi* in œil, an eye, or *eui* in fauteuil, an arm-chair.

e is like English *e* in set, let.

ei and *ey* are like English *ei* in eight or *ai* in wait.

i and *y* answer to *i* in fit, or *y* final as in country, misery, &c.

í and *ý* are like to *ee* in free or *ea* in steam.

o is like open English *o* in spot or *aw* in law.

ó is like English closed *o* in pole, mote, or *oa* in coal, or *ow* in low.

u has no approximately resembling sound in English. It sounds very like the final *u* in the name of the well-known author Lefanu, and comes still nearer to the French *u* in certain combinations; f. e. in *tuera* (*tu ne tueras pas*), fut. of *tuer* to slay.

ú is like *u* in true or *oo* in pool.

æ and *œ* sound like *i* in fine.

CONSONANTS.

b, d, k, v, are pronounced as in English.

ð is like English soft *th* when followed by an *e* mute, as in breathe (never like *th* in mother or brother).

f commencing a word is pronounced as in English; final or between two vowels it sounds like *v*, haf = hav, lifa = liva.

g has two sounds, hard and soft. Hard, like *g* initial in English, in the beginning of words and when doubled, as in gall, gráta, gefa, geta, hregg, rugga; and final (= Engl. *g* final in monosyllables like bog, leg, wig, &c.) when preceded by a consonant, as berg, elg, eng. Its soft sound lies between a guttural and a palatal, like the Danish *g* in bog, and resembles the German *g* in tag. This sound, which *g* has lost in Swedish and English—where it has gravitated into *w*, as in sag-a, to saw, &c., or into *y*, as in veg-r = way—it has in Icelandic: (1), final, after an open vowel and í, au, ey, ei, as in lag, log, síg, beyg, laug, veig; (2), after an open vowel and í, au, ei, when followed by open vowel, ð, r, s, or t, as in laga, loga, logum, sígum, laugum, veigum, vígð, hnígr, vígs, vígt, &c. This letter is never an aspirate in Icelandic. It is mute when preceded by á, ó, ú, (nóg, lág = nó, lá), likewise where, in this case, it is followed by an open vowel: hrúga = hrúa, bóga = bóa. Followed by *i* or *j*, its sound is swamped into a *j*; f. e. svigi = sviji, bagi = baji, logi = loji.

h is merely an aspirate, as in English in words of Northern origin.

j is sounded as *y* consonant in English.

l, *m*, *n*, *p*, in commencing a word, sound as in English. Within, and at the end of a word, they sound as the same letters in English, when followed by an *e* mute. Double, they sound as the same letters do in English, with the exception of

ll, between two vowels and final, sounding like ddl, as kalla (= kaddla), to call, öll (= öddl) all, and

nn, which sounds after closed vowel sounds (with a few exceptions) like *ddn:* einn = eiddn, grœnn = grœddn, sveinn = sveiddn, &c.

r sounds as *r* initial in English, never as English *r* final; rn=ddn, barn=baddn, stjarna=stjaddna.

s and *z* sound always like hard *s* in English.

x sounds always as soft *g* + *s* = eghs, never as *x* in English.

þ is like English hard *th* in think, but with a broader aspiration.

ABBREVIATIONS.

acc. accusative.
ad. adjective.
adv. adverb.
collect. collective.
comparat. comparative.
conj. conjunction.
dat. dative.
dual. and *d.* dual number.
f. feminine gender.
f. indecl. and *ind.* feminine indeclinable.
f. pl. feminine plural.
gen. genitive.
id. the same.
imperat. imperative.
imperf. and *imp.* imperfect.
impers. impersonal.
ind. indicative mood.
Lat. Latin.
loc. local.
m. masculine gender.
n. neuter gender.
n. pl. neuter plural.
nom. nominative.
num. card. cardinal number.
num. ord. ordinal number.
pa. participle active.
pl. plural number.
poss. possessive.
pp. past participle.
prep. preposition.
pron. dem., *indef.*, *interr.*, *refl.*, *relat.*, pronoun demonstrative, indefinite, interrogative, reflexive, relative.
sing. singular number.
subj. subjunctive.
superlat. superlative.
temp. temporal.
v. a. active verb.
v. n. neuter verb.

CORRIGENDA.

Page 4, 9, read 'væri' for 'vœri.'
5, 6, place a comma after 'lips.'
8, note, read 'plausible' for 'feasible.'
10, 18, read 'fiska ok fugla' for 'fugla ok fiska.'
28, 6, read 'Sjöfalds' for 'sjöfalds.'
30, and elsewhere, read 'júngfrú' for 'jungfrú.'
48, 6, read 'þeygi' for 'þeigi.'
52, 9, read 'knè' for 'hnè.'
55, and elsewhere, read 'Mær' for 'mær.'
62, after 'B.R.' at the end of the Latin citations, add '1629.'
67, 4, read 'didst thou think' for 'deemed'st thou.'
68, 9, read 'hœfi' for 'hœfi'.'
89, note, after 'mites fac et castos' add the citation: 'Ave maris stella. *Brev. Rom.* 1551, 577. '
100, 5, read 'ok' for 'á.'
100, 14, read 'valdi,' for 'valdi;'
101, 5, read 'and' for 'in.'
105, read 'p.p.' after 'blásinn' for 'pa.'
108, read 'n. pl.' after 'feðgin' for 'n. indecl.'
123, after 'þá, adv. temp.' add 'then;'
124, read 'æðr (-ar, -ar)' for 'æðr (-ar,–)'

LILJA—THE LILY.

LILJA.

1.

Almáttigr Guð allrar stèttar,
Yfir-bjóðandinn engla ok þjóða,
Ei þurfandi staða nè stunda,
Stað haldandi í kyrrleiks valdi,
Senn verandi úti ok inni,
Uppi ok niðri, ok þar í miðju,
Lof sè þèr um aldr ok æfi,
Eining sönn í þrennum greinum.

2.

Œski ek þína mikla miskun
Mèr veitir, ef ek eftir leita
Klökkum hug, því at innist ekki
Annat gott, en af þèr til, Drottinn.
Hreinsaðu brjóst, ok leið með listum
Lífleg orð í stuðla-skorðum,
Steflig gjörð at vísan verði
Vunnin yðr af þessum munni.

---

1. 1. Allra stètta, A.—3. Staða, so altered by the editor; staði, B.; staði nè stundir, A.

2. 1. Þín hin m, A.—2. Veitir, my conjecture; veitist, B; veitist, er ek, &c. A.—5. Hreinsað,

THE LILY.

1.

Almighty God of every state,
Who angels rulest, and nations' fate,
Who needest neither place nor hour,
Abiding in thy tranquil power,
At once abroad, and yet within,
Above, below, and there between,
Through ages everlastingly
Be praised, O One in Trinity.

2.

Grant me, I pray, thy mercy great,
With humble heart I thee entreat;
For, Father, from thine hand alone,
The source of all my bliss I own:
Oh, cleanse my heart, let it rehearse
Rejoicing words in measured verse;
Then for thy glory shall my tongue
Bring thee a shapely burthen song.

B; hreinsa, A.—7. Stefnlig gjörð svá, A.—8. A's text begins with 'af þessum munni' in the first line of fol. 25.

3.

Beiði ek þik, Mær ok Móðir,
Mínum at fyrir umsján þína
Renni mál af raddar tólum
Rèttferðugast í vísum slèttum ;
Skýr ok sœt af vörum vórum
Vorðin, svá at mælti forðum,
Laugist öll í glóanda gulli ;
Guði vœri ek þau skyldr at fœra.

4.

Fyrri menn, at frœðin kunnu
Forn ok klók af heiðnum bókum,
Slúngin mjúkt af sínum kóngum
Súngu lof með danskri túngu ;
Af þvílíku móður-máli
Meirr skyldumst, enn nokkurr þeirra,
Hrœrðan dikt með ástar orðum
Allsvaldanda kungi at gjalda.

---

3. 5. Vorum vörum, A.—6. Vorðin svá at mætti orðin | laugast, *i.e. enata ut verba tingerentur*, B and the editions, out-taken that of 'Hin gamla Vijsnabook, Hoolum, 1612,' which reads, 'orðin þau sem mæltust forðum | laugaðist,' *i.e.* 'that the words which were spoken of old might be bathed,' &c. The v in vorðin (qs. v-orðin) is merely a prothesis by way of poetic license, in order to satisfy the law of alliterative attraction between the 'stuðlar' (the metric stays) of line 5, vör-, vór-, and the so-called 'head-letter' (the letter which commences every second line in a couplet) of line 6 ; cpr. En at verðleikrinn

3

Thee, May and Mother, I entreat,
That by thine intercession sweet
From out my mouth a truthful lore
In verses smoothly wrought may pour;
That from my lips both soft and bright,
As if in glowing gold bedight,
The words proclaimed of old may ring;
To God that gift I needs must bring.

4.

The former men, who drew their lore
From heathen books in days of yore,
Sang many a smooth and praiseful song
About their kings in Danish tongue;
In that same language I emprise,
On whom a holier duty lies,
A song in lovesome speech to bring
Devoutly to my heavenly King.

---

víss á jörðu | *vyrði*, for yrði, 14, 1-2. The corruption of the text has been brought about in the following manner: vorðin, which the reader mistook for neut. plur. nom., past-part. of verða, *Germ.* werden, to become, required some noun to which to be referred, forming the subject of laugast; and as the verse contained no such noun, the unintelligible forðum was soon changed into orðin, and in the train of that change went forthwith that of mælti to mætti (might) and laugist to laugast. — 7. Laugist, my alteration; laugast, A. B.

4. 2. Sínum bók., B.— 3. Súngu mjúkt, A.— 5. 'I þvíliku,' &c.— 6. Skyldast ek, A.

5.

Skapan ok fœðing, skírn ok prýði,
Skynsemd full, at betri er gulli,
Dreyrinn Krists af síðu-sári,
Synda-líkn, ok dagligt yndi,
Háleit von á himna sælu,
Hrygðin jarðar neðstu bygðar,
Bjóða mèr í frásögn fœra
Fögr stórmerkin Drottins verka.

6.

Herra Guð, sá hverjum er dýrri,
Himin ok jörð í fyrstu gjörði,
Prýddi hann með þrisvar þrennum—
Það er rètt trú mín—engla-stèttum.
Áður var hann, jafnt ok síðan,
Œrinn sèr, en skepnan væri;
Gjörði hann heim, ok teygði tíma,
Tvá jafnaldra í sínu valdi.

5. This strophe gives a paraphrastic abstract of Beda's summary of the contents of the songs of Cædmon: '*Canebat autem de creatione mundi, et origine humani generis . . . . de aliis plurimis sacræ scripturæ historiis, de incarnatione domini, ac passione, et resurrectione et ascensione in cælum, de adventu spiritus sancti, et apostolorum doctrina. Item de terrore futuri judicii et horrore pœnæ gehennalis et dulcedine regni cælestis multa carmina faciebat;*' *i. e.* But he sang of the creation of the world, and of the origin of mankind . . . . and of many other stories of sacred scripture;

5.

The shapen world, man's beauty, birth,
His baptism, wit beyond gold's worth,
The blood from Jesus' side that ran,
Redemption, daily joy of man;
The hope of heaven's eternal bliss,
The tortures of earth's low abyss:
These wonders bid me to record
In song thy beauteous works, O Lord.

6.

The Lord, above all things in worth,
Created erst both heaven and earth,
With angel orders thrice threefold
He that adorned—such faith I hold.
Yet he was still, as heretofore,
God all sufficing evermore.
The world he made and measured hour,
The twin-aged offspring of his power.

---

of the incarnation of the Lord, and his passion and resurrection and ascension into heaven; of the coming of the Holy Ghost, and of the teaching of the apostles. Likewise, of the terrors of future judgment, and the horrors of hell's punishment, and of the sweetness of the heavenly kingdom, made he many songs. *Beda, Hist. Ecc.* l. iv. ch. xxiv. — 1. Sköpun, A. — 2. Skynsemi f. er betri en gullit, A.—5. Von er á, &c. A.—8. Stórmerki, A.

6. 4. Engla-stéttar, B.—5. Jafn, B.

7.

Mektar-fullur af þar öllum
Í náttúru-skærleik sínum,
Skapaðr góðr, ok skein í prýði,
Skapara næstr í vegsemd hæstri;
Eigi lèt sèr alla nœgjast
Engill makt at hafði fengit,
Með ofbeldi öðlast vildi
Œðri sess ok virðing bæði.

8.

Fýstist hann með ofsa œstum
At viðrlíkjast yfrið ríkum
Guðs eingetnum Syni, síðan
Sèr nœgjandi en engu vægja,
Fúll metnaðrinn er með öllu,
Óvarliga, sem ritning prófar,
Ætlar sèr við dýran Drottin
Deila megn. En hversu vegnar?

7. The seventh stanza seems to come so abruptly in here—and yet there is no other place to assign to it in the poem—that one cannot help thinking that what it alludes to must have originally formed the subject of a stanza preceding it. Mektarfullur refers to one, who as yet is unnamed, as does öllum to the angels who have not yet come in for treatment in the poem, when we except the engla-stèttir in the preceding stanza, to which öllum cannot refer naturally. It seems, therefore, feasible that the original stanza, enumerating and describing, after the manner of the old hexaëmerons, the nine orders of the angels, and Lucifer as the chief of the disobedient band, may be lost, a supposition which is strengthened by the fact that the poem, properly speaking, is now only ninety-nine stanzas long. Or is it to be supposed that the stanza, though begun, was never finished by the poet, and therefore dropped out of the MSS. of 'The Lily?' It is

7.

An angel of exceeding might,
Excelled his race in nature bright;
Made good, he shone in beauty's beam,
Next to his Lord in high esteem;
But all the angelic might decreed
To him he deemed beneath his meed,
On loftier place, more glorious name,
In wanton pride he fixed his aim.

8.

In wild presumption, passing bound,
He fain would be the equal found
Of God's dear only Son—and thought
Thus self-reliant to yield to nought—
When reckless pride did dare engage,
As clearly proves the sacred page,
With God Almighty to contend.
But, mark ye, whereto came his end?

---

certainly strange that in a poem of such popularity there should be no MS. extant to show traces of that stanza if it ever got into the current copies of the song.—2. Náttúru ok, A.—5. Allvel nœgja, A.—6. Engils, A.

8. 1-8. 'Þá es hann sá sik öllum englum œðra í dýrð ok fegurð, þá fyr leit hann þat allt, ok vildi vesa jafn sem Goð eða meiri . . . œðri tign vildi hann taka af nauðgum Goði, en Goð gaf honum, at ráða öðrom fyr ofríke. Discipulus: Hvat gerðesk þá?' *i.e.* 'Whenas he saw himself above all angels in glory and beauty, he scorned all that, and would be equal to God or greater still . . . . he would wrench from God a higher dignity than God had given to him, namely, to rule others by tyranny. Discipulus: What befell then? Elucid. 12, 9-15.—3. Syni, en síðan, B.—5. Metn. óx með ö, A.—6. Ofrlega, A.—7. Hann ætlar, A.—8. Deil mega, A.; vegr, A.

9.

Svá er greinanda, á sömu stundu
Sem engillinn tók at spillast,
Söktist hann, með sínum grönnum,
Sem blý-varða, í djúpleik jarðar;
Blindan þar sem föðr sinn, fjandann,
Feikt ofbeldit kvelr í eldi;
Fávíss er sá, eð feðgin þessi
Faðma vill, en siðunum spilla.

10.

Dœgrin sex at vísu vuxu
Veltilig um upp-hafs belti,
Aðr en fengi alla prýði
Jörð ok loft, þat er Drottinn gjörði:
Pressat vatn í himininn hvassa,
Hjörn ok eld, sem merki-stjörnur,
Haglig dýr, sem fugla ok fiska,
Fagran plóg, sem aldin-skóga.

9. 1. Greinandi í samri, A.—1-4. Perhaps a reminiscence of Elucid. 12, 15, 13, 5, cpr. Elucid. 8, 7, 9, 5.—5. Fann þar föðr, A.—6. Feikna ofb. kvelst, A.—7. Fáv. varð enn, A.—8. Ok siðum, A.

10. 2. Vellteleg um siófarb.

9.

The very hour, the story says,
That he took to his evil ways,
He and his worthless comrades fell,
Like lead, cast down to lowest hell:
Rebellion there torments its sire,
The fiend, in never dying fire.
How foolish he, who such a kin
Befriends, to swell the bale of sin.

10.

Six days and nights revolving went
Through high zones of the firmament,
Ere all bedecked in beauty were
The new created earth and air:
With water, driven through windy sky,
With ice, and fire, and star signs high,
With shapely beasts, fish, fowl untold,
With fair grown fields, and fruitful wold.

B.—4. Loft sem d. A.—5. Pressast, A.—6. Eldr. B; Merki ok st. A.—7. Hagl ok, A. B. and editions; haglig, the undoubted original reading, I borrow from the Vijsnabook, cited above.

11.

Breytti Guð, ok brá til hætti,
Blóð ok hold af vatni ok moldu,
Lèttan blástr af lofti næsta,
Ok lífs heitleika af sólar reitum,
Önd ok þar til síðan sendi,
Sú er skiljandi Drottins vilja,
Leið kunnandi um líkams æðar,
Líf skínandi af Helgum Anda.

12.

Svá er líðandi maðr af móður
Moldu, þó er með skæru holdi,
Adam nefndr, eð alls í heimi
Atti ráð með frelsi ok náðum.
Höfginn rann svá hœgr á þenna
Heims-stýranda, ok fèkk hann skýra
Andagift, þá er síðan sýndi,
Svá vorðinna spádóms-orða.

11. 2-7. 'Hann hafðe hold of jörðo, enn blóð af vatne, blóst af lofte, enn hita af elde;' *i.e.* 'He had flesh of earth, but blood of water, breath of air, but heat of fire.' Elucid. 19, 10-12. 'Ok hefer hon (*i.e.* önd) skilning . . . . en hon má í gegnom fara alla sýnelega hlute;' *i.e.* 'and she has (*i.e.* the soul) understanding . . . . but she may penetrate all visible things. Elucid. 20, 15, 21, 5.—3. Leittan, B. — 6. Svo er skiljanda, B.

12. 2. Moldu ok þó með, A.— 3. Eð om., A.—3, 4, 6. 'I því hafðe hann ok glíking Goðs at hann skylde svá stýra öllo á jörðo, sem Goð ræðr öllo á himne;' *i.e.* 'Therein had he too the likeness of God, that he was to rule all things on earth, in the same manner as God rules all

11.

And next, by varied mode of make,
Of mould and water God did take
Man's flesh and blood, his breath from air,
His life's warmth from the sun's ways fair;
And unto these he added still
A soul, to know his holy will,
And through man's fleshly life to shine,
Resplendent with a light divine.

12.

Though sprung from dust, with earthly shroud
Of bright flesh Adam was endowed,
That first man, who in freedom's ease
Ruled all the earth in fearless peace:
This swayer of earth, in slumbers light
A-fallen, had a vision bright
Unveiled to him, whereof he spoke
In prophecies when he awoke.

---

things in heaven.' Elucid, 22, 7-9. —4. Atti at ráða með, A.—6. Heims stýrandans fèkk, A.; hann, om., B.—6-8. These verses, which are doubtless corrupt, are meant to express the following words of Elucidarius: 'Goðs ande nam hann upp í himneska paradísu ok sá hann þá þat at Kristus ok sancta Kristne mönde berask ór hans kyne, því spáðe hann of þau þegar es hann vagnaðe;' *i.e.* 'God's spirit took him up into the heavenly Paradise, and then he saw that Christ and holy Christianity would be born of his kin, therefore he prophesied concerning them forthwith as he awoke.' Elucid. 24, 15, 22, 1.—7. Þá síðan sendi, A.; ok fèkk hann skírar | Andagiftir síðan sendar, Vijsnabook.

13.

Út leiðandi af Adams síðu
Evam brátt, sem Moyses váttar,
Víst með æru, vald ok ástir,
At vísu gaf hann þeim Paradísar,
Þangat til er þau með englum—
Þat er blíðan mest—lifði síðan,
Með afsprengi, allt þat fengi,
Æfinlega, ok þakkir gæfi.

14.

En at verðleikrinn víss á jörðu
Vyrði sök til himna dýrðar,
Boðorðit eitt enn blíði Drottinn
Býður þeim í skyldu at hlýða:
'Eplit eitt ek banna at bíta
Báðum ykkr, en þið munut ráða;
Deyja skulut, ef efnit eigi
Einfalt boð með dyggleik hreinum.'

13. 2. Evu . . . Moses, A.—3. Vist, A. (víst = vist).—4-8. Seem vaguely to represent the following passage of Elucidarius: 'Discipulus: Hverso lenge skyldo menn vesa í Paradíso? Magister: Unðz fylldesk tala þeirra engla es fórosk ok sú tala heilagra es fyllask skyllde í paradíso, þó at englar föresk eigi. Ok svá sem nú berask aðrer í stað, es aðrer deyja, svá möndo ok þá feðr vesa upp numner til betre vista, síðan es þeir bergðe af lífs trè, en síðan hverr áttboge effter annan á fyrer-ætlaðre tíð, en at næst möndo aller saman verða jafner sem englar á himne.' *i.e.* 'D.: How long should man be in Paradise? M.: Until the number should be fulfilled of the angels who were lost, and until the number of the holy ones

13.

Then God led Eve from Adam's side,
As Moses says, and bade them bide
In honour, power, and loving wise,
Within their home of Paradise,
Till with the angels' holy race
They should be joined in better place,
With all their kin, a life to spend
Of sweet thanksgiving without end.

14.

But that by merit, earned on earth,
Man might become for heaven worth,
The Lord, all gracious, doth demand
Obedience to this sole command :—
'One fruit I bid that both of ye
Forbear—yet let your will be free :
If ye in faith sincere do not
Keep this command, be death your lot.'

should be filled which was to be filled in Paradise, even if no angels had been lost; and whereas some are born forthwith as others die off, so the fathers should be taken up into better abodes when they had tasted of the tree of life, and then each generation after the other at the predestined time, and at last all should be equal to the angels in heaven. Elucid.

26. 4-15.—4. At vísug af þeim, A.—5. Til eru, A.—6. Þá er blíðan mist er lifðu, A.—7. Adopted from *Hist. Ecc.;* meðan afsprengrinn, A.; v'ðr afs'png̅ (viðr afsprengi?) alt þat er fengi, B.

14. 1. Sem verðleikrinn vóx, A.—2. At irðe, A.—3. Boð. lèt fram blíður, B.—5. Epli er eitt, A.

15.

Þrútnar, svellr, ok unir vit illa
Engill bann, þat er hafði fengit,
Fyrða sveitin, fœdd á jörðu,
Fái þar vist, er sjálfr hann misti;
Ok bruggandi dauðans dreggjar,
Duldist hann fyrir augsjón manna,
Fjölkunnugr í einum innan
Ormi tók hann mál at forma.

16.

Sem prófandi segir til Evu—
'Svara mèr skjótt, en hví hefir Dróttinn
Sœtast ykkur blóm at bíta
Bannat, en lofat flest allt annat?'
Svá fór þat, er svaraði Eva
Sem marg-brugðinn fjandinn hugði:
'At við eigi lífs af leiðum
Lèttliga hröpum á dauðans stèttir.'

15. 1-4. 'Fyrir hví sveik djöfull þau? Mag.: Því at hann övundaðe þau es þau skyldo koma til þess vegs es hann vas frá rekenn fyr ofmetnoð;' *i.e.* 'Why did the devil deceive them? Master: Because he envied them that they should succeed to that honour from which he was driven for the

15.

Now swelled that angel's bitter gall,
Who laden with dire curse did fall,
To think, that man, an earth born host,
Should gain the home that he had lost;
Thus, brewing dregs of death, a guise
He took deceiving human eyes,
And, crafty, in a creeping worm
He thus began his speech to form.

16.

To Eve he speaks this tempting word—
'Why, tell me, prithee, has the Lord
Forbidden you this fruit most sweet,
But all things else allowed to eat?'
And so it fell, the woman wrought
Her answer as the fiend had thought—
'Lest from life's path, by easy slide,
E'en into traps of death we glide.'

sake of his pride.' *Elucid.* 27, 14-16; cpr. 21, 12-17.—3. Sveitin er fœdd, A.—5. Senn brugg., A. —6. Augsýn, A.—8. Tók svá, A.

16. 1. Svá, A.—2. En því hefir A.—4. Lofat en flestallt, B.; en lof. gjörvallt, A.—5. At svar, A. 7. At ei fari við lífs, B.; að vèr eigum, A.—8. Lèttlega hrapa á, A.

17.

Lèttliga fann þar svá ljósin váttar,
Lèttleikann í svaranna reikan;
Því treystist hann framt at freista,
Flærðum settr, ok talar með prettum —
'Eigi munu þið Adam deyja,
Andlits-hvít, þó at eplit bítið,
Heldur munut með heiðri ok valdi
Horsk ok rík við guðdóm líkjast.'

18.

Auðginnt mjök því Eva trúði,
At hún blóm, en tapaði sóma,
Ok þar með sèr Adam teygði,
Vann nú þat, er vissi bannat;
Ugði hann at Eva stygðist,
Ef neitaði hann bœn at veita.
Fjandinn gat svá fyrstu blindað
Feðgin vár með nœgu dári.

17. 1. Fann svá ljósan vott-inn, A.—2. Lèttleika, B.—reiki, A.—5. Munuð, A.

18. 3. Ok til með, A.—5. Evam (stygði?), B.—7. I fyrstu bundit, A.

17.

Forthwith the clearest note he heard
Of lightness in her wavering word,
And, fraught with craft, his tempting wile
He boldly urged, and spake with guile—
'Ye, fair of face, heed nought that tale;
To eat the fruit can work no bale;
Nay, but in honour and power arrayed,
Like God himself ye shall be made.'

18.

The simple Eve was moved by this
To eat the fruit, and forfeit bliss;
And Adam, too, she did persuade
To do that which their God forbade:
For fear she might grow wroth thereby
This boon he nowise would deny;
And thus the fiend did first beguile
Our parents with exceeding wile.

19.

Refsar þeim at rèttum dómi
Ríkur Guð fyrir ódygð slíka,
Rak þau braut af sœmdar sæti,
Snauð ok nökt, í myrkr ok dauða.
Veltust aum í veslum heimi,
Víða lands þar er nær öll síðan
Lýða kind af sárum syndum
Sendist fram af Adams lendum.

20.

Remman brast af rót í kvistu,
Rann þá glœpr af hverjum til annars;
Leið svá heimr um langan tíma
Lífs andvani, ok fullr af grandi;
Lèttir hvorki ugg nè ótta,
Eftir mest en þó er at lesti:
Opit helvíti, búit með bölvi,
Bauð sik fram við hvers manns dauða.

19. 2. R. herra, B.—4. I písl ok, A.—5. Veltust um, A.—6. Er, om. in A.—7. Með sárum s., A.

20. 1. Sem rót á kvistum, A.—4. Andvana, A.—5. Leittir, B.—6. En eitt er mest sem þó er, A.

19.

This faithless deed the mighty Lord
Did punish with a just award,
And drave them, naked, far away
From bliss, for plague and death a prey:
They wallowed in this world of woe,
And wide as earth's far borders go
From Adam's loins the human kin
Sprang forth in pain and grievous sin.

20.

As bitter sap from root to branch,
So spread now crime that none might stanch;
Thus sped the world, with ruin rife,
Through ages long, devoid of life:
There was no ease from dread or fear,
But this its worst fruit sin did bear,
That baleful hell stood open wide,
A-gape for every man that died.

21.

Heimr er dauðr, en hvat er ráða?
Hvar getr þann, er sèr megi bjarga?
Hvergi; því at í synda saurgan
Sannlega hverr at þyngir annan.
Eitt er til, þat er ek skal vátta,
A ek grátandi frammi at standa,
Attú sjálfr, enn dýri Drottinn,
Dugir nú ferð, svá lífgut verði.

22.

Veitt er líf, þat er varð er mátti,
Veitt er líf, þat er Adam neitti;
Sú miskunn á settum tíma
Sendist fram af guðdóms hendi:
Ljós í heim at lifanda kœmi,
Lifandi víst, en kvaldar andir
Tæki á braut úr djöfla díki;
Dýrð englanna slíku stýrði.

---

21. 1. Dauðr hvat er ráða, A. —4. Sannar þat at hverr, B — 5. Þat ek vil votta, A.—7. Au þú sjálfr, B.—8. Dugi.

21.

The world is dead. What shall be done?
Who may his own life save? Not one:
For each doth drag the other in
'Mid all contaminating sin:
In tears I must stand forth, and say
How man is saved in but one way:
That thou, O Lord, in pity give
Thy blessed aid, that all may live.

22.

To us, in fitting season born,
Was given the life that man did scorn;
In time fulfilled this mercy great
God sent to right our wretched state:
That living light should come below
To set the souls which lived in woe
From out the devil's dungeon free;
Such was the angel-king's decree.

22nd stanza = the 23rd in B.—1. Ok mátti, A.—5. Ljòs í heiminn at lifandi, A.—6. Ok kvaldar, B.—7. Tak (?) burt, B.

23.

Tendrast öll ok tala með snilli,
Túnga mín, af Herra þínum,
Um stórmerkin áttu at yrkja
Yfir-spennandans heima þrennra;
Bjúg ok sár í banni værir
Ok bandi rètt ens neðsta fjanda,
Nema hjálpræði Guðs hit góða,
Gefit á jörð, mik leystan hefði.

24.

Nær ok firr með skygnleik skýrum
Skapandi allt með Syni ok Anda,
Föðr-persóna engli einum
Erindit býðr, en þessi hlýðir —
'Fljúg, ok seg þat Maríu Meyju
Mætri, þeirri er ek skal gæta,
Minn Einka-son holdi hennar
Hlýðinnar vill björtu skrýðast.'

23, the 22nd in B.—1. Talar, A.—2. Túngan mín . . . sínum, A.—3. A ek at yrkja, A.—4. Þrenna, A.—5. Bjúgr ok sárr i b, væri A; í bandi v., B.—6. Ok, om. in B.—7. Utan hjálpin Guðs hins góða, A.—8. Gefin . . . . verði, A.

24. 1. Skærleik skýrum, A.—2-8. Cpr. '*Deus, qui de beatæ*

23.

My tongue, let fiery grow thy word,
Extol in graceful strain thy Lord,
His wondrous works thou art to praise,
Who holds three worlds in one embrace;
All bent thou wert 'neath ban and woe,
And bonds of that infernal foe,
Had not my God's salvation free
Been sent on earth to ransom me.

24.

Swaying with clear pervading eye
All things afar, all things anigh,
With Son and Ghost, the Father blest
To Gabriel gave this high behest:
'Unto the dear May, Mary, fly—
With whom my watch and ward aby—
Tell her, my only Son doth yearn
Him with her bright flesh to adorn.'

Virginis Mariæ utero, verbum tuum angelo nuntiante, carnem suscipere voluisti;' i.e. 'God, who by the annunciation of thy word through the angel, didst desire to assume the flesh from the womb of the blessed Virgin Mary,' &c. *Brev. Rom.* 1551, 577. 3. Feðr personar, B.—4. Erindit, A.—6. Ek vil gæta, A.

25.

Móðir oss er María þessi,
Mektar-blóm, en full af sóma,
Glœsileg, sem roðnut rósa,
Runnin upp við lifandi brunna;
Rót ilmandi lítillætis,
Logandi öll með skýrleiks Anda,
Guði unnandi ok góðum mönnum,
Guði líkjandi í dygðum slíkum.

26.

FYRRI STEFJA-MAL.

Engin sè ek at jarðlig túnga,
Enn háleiti stjörnu-reitar
Drottinn, þèr, sem verðugt væri,
Vandat fái nú stef til handa—

FYRRA STEF.

Sè þèr dýrð með sannri prýði,
Súnginn heiðr af öllum túngum
Eilíflega, með sigri ok sælu,
Sœmd ok vald þitt minkist aldri.

---

25. 2. Ok full, A.—3. Sem rjóðust, A., cpr. '*Quid dicemus de te, O præclara mater inter mulieres? si rosam te dixerimus, floridior es, &c.*;' *i.e.* 'What shall we say of thee, O excellent mother among women? if we call thee a rose, thou art more blooming still, &c.' *St. Bernard, Tractatus ad laudem gloriosæ V. Matris.*—8. Guð líkj., B.; guði líkust, A.

25.

This Mary is our mother bright,
With honour decked, a flower of might,
And bloometh like a ruddy rose,
Which by a living fountain grows;
A fragrant root of lowliness,
A ray of the Spirit's holiness;
She loves but God and who are good,
In virtue is she like to God.

26.

THE FIRST STAVE-LAY.

Nought know I how a tongue of earth
May bring thee any song of worth,
Lord of the star-realm, though it were
Wrought for thy praising with all care—

FIRST STAVE.

Thy honour and thy bliss be sung,
Thy praise resound from every tongue,
Thy glory all triumphant be,
Thy power abide eternally.

---

26. The headings — Fyrri stefja-mál, Fyrra stef, Stef, Síðari stefjamál, Síðara stef, Stef—are added by the editor throughout.

1-2. Engi segi jardnesk túnga
Ok ei háleitur stjörnu-reitur, A.—5. Af sannri p., B.—7. Æfinlega með s., B.

27.

Leið, sigrandi páfugls prýði,
Pentat innan firmamentum,
Gabríel, sem geisli sólar,
Gleðiligr, í loft hin neðri.
Sendiboði kom sjöfalds Anda,
Svá er greinandi, at húsi einu,
Sannur meydómr sat þar inni,
Sjálft hreinlífit, gimsteinn vífa.

28.

Ok svá veik at meyju mjúkri—
'María, hlýð nú orðum várum,
Frægast víf, þèr fœri ek ave,
Full miskunnar sœtleiks brunna;
Samangeypnandi sína skepnu
Sannur höfðinginn engla ok manna,
Byggir þèr fyrir brjósti skæru,
Blessut Mær, þú ert sprundum hærri!'

27. 5. Sendiboðinn, A.—6. Greinat, B.
28. 2. Hlýð þú, A.—4. '*Ave, Maria, gratia plena*,' Vulgate Luc. 1, 28.—5. Samangaupnandi sínar skepnur, A.—5-7. cpr.:

27.

Excelling all a peacock's sheen,
Through radiant firmament, I ween,
The angel Gabriel glad doth fare,
Like sunbeam, toward the lower air:
The sevenfold Spirit's messenger
Came to a house, the tales aver,
Where the chaste Maiden sat within,
The purest gem of woman kin.

28.

To the sweet May, then, drawing near,
He spake :—'Deign thou my words to hear;
Thee, Maid of wondrous grace, I greet,
Be filled with joy from fountains sweet;
The Lord who holds in one embrace
All creatures, men, and angels' race,
Abideth 'neath thy spotless breast,
'Mong women favoured, Maiden blest!'

'Beata mater munere,
Cujus supernus artifex
Mundum pugillo continens
Ventris sub arca clausus est.'

Offic. Beatæ Mariæ, Brev. Rom. 1551, fol. 576.—s. Þú ert englum, A.

29.

Heyrði ok trúði, en undrast orðin,
Jungfrú kyrr, því vissi hún fyrri,
Aldri kvaddan mann á moldu
Með þvílíkri tignar-kveðju.
Fyrirbjóðandi henni at hræðast,
Höfuð-engillinn talaði lengur—
'Guð himnanna fram mun fœðast,
Frúin skínandi, af holdi þínu.'

30.

Frèttir nú, með hverjum hætti
Henni bœri til fögnut þenna,
Borgar-múr svá at brysti hvergi
Bygð geymandi hreinleiks dygða.
Engill segir, at ei mun syndga
Jungfrú blíð, þótt sveininn smíði
Hagleiks-mundin Heilags Anda,
Hold ok bein af líkam hreinum.

29. 1. Ok undrast, A.—2. Júngfrúin kær, A.—3. Frumskínandi, B.; af lífi, A.

30. 1. Hún frèttir, A.—5. At ei muni spillast, A.—6. Þá er sveinn er smíðaðr, B.—7. Haglig myndan, B.—8. Líkama, A.

29.

This heard, believed, but marvelled sore
The gentle May, for none before
She knew addressed of folk a-mould
With majesty so manifold.
Forbidding her to fear in aught,
The angel further message brought—
'O Lady, undefiled and fair,
The God of heaven thy womb shall bear.'

30.

She asked, then, by what mode withal
Such joy might unto her befall,
Without the breaking of the fold
Which all pure chastity doth hold:
The angel said, nowise defiled
The sweet May should become, the child
Being shapen of her flesh and bone
By the Holy Spirit's power alone.

31.

Loftin öll af ljósi fyllast,
Legir á grundu stóðu ok undrast,
Kúguð sjálf svo nærri nógu
Náttúran sèr ekki mátti.
Giftist öndin guðdóms krafti
Góð, ok huldist Maríu blóði;
Glaðrar dvelst í júngfrúr iðrum
Ein persóna þrennrar greinar.

32.

Hjörtun játi, falli ok fljóti
Fagnaðar-laug af hvers manns augum,
Æ þakkandi miskun mikla,
Minn Drottinn, í holdgan þinni—

STEF.

Sè þèr dýrð með sannri prýði,
Súnginn heiðr af öllum túngum
Eilíflega, með sigri ok sælu,
Sœmd ok vald þitt minkist aldri.

---

31. 2. A grund þá st. A.—3. Af nærri n. B.—5-8.:
,*Perfusa cœli gratia*
Gestant puellæ viscera;
Trinam regentem machinam
Claustrum Mariæ baiulat.'

Ave Maria Hymnus, Brev. Rom.

31.

With glorious light all heavens fill,
And wonderstruck all waters still
Their course on earth. In powerless way
Self nature all prostrated lay.
The soul, wed to the power of God,
Was shrouded in good Mary's blood;
In the favoured Virgin's womb doth lie
He who is One in Trinity.

32.

Let hearts confess, let fall and flow
From all eyes tears of joy enow,
With thanks that God, in mercy great,
Was flesh to mend our fallen state—

STAVE.

Thine honour and thy bliss be sung,
Thy praise resound from every tongue,
Thy glory all triumphant be,
Thy power abide eternally.

1551, fol. 576.—8. Þrennra greina, A.

32. 1. Fagni ok fl, A.—4. Fyrir holdgan þ., B.; í hèrvist þ., A.—5-8. Cpr. note on strophe 26; of the 'stef' only the first three words are given in B.

33.

Fimm mánuðum ok fjórum síðar
Fœðist sveinn af meyju hreinni,
Skygnast sem þá glerið gegnum
Geislinn brár fyrir augum várum;
Glór, sem sól at glerinu heilu,
Gleðilegt jóð, er skínn af móður,
At innsigli höldnu hennar
Hreinferðugra meydóms greina.

34.

Engin heyrðust, engin urðu
Jöfn tíðindin fyrr nè síðar,
Bæði senn, því mær ok móðir
Mann ok Guð bauð trúna at sanna.
Loftin súngu komnum kóngi
Kunnigt lof, þar hirðar runnu.
Himna dýrð er hneigð á jörðu,
Hèr samtengdust menn ok englar.

33. 1. Ok om. in B.; síðan, A.—3. Sem þar (= þá er?), B.—5. Glóar þar sól af gl. B.; sem is adopted from Vijsnabook; glór þar sól á glerinu, A.—6. Jóðit skínn, B.; skein, A.—8. Hreinferðugastra, B.

34. 1. Enginn heyrði ok e., A,—3. Því at mær, A.—4. Mann ok Guð bauð trúan at s., B. I have great doubts about A's reading, but it seems, in any case, preferable to B's, if we can explain 'mann' and 'Guð' as datives, with the terminal *i* apocopated, cpr. 59, 7, týndu

33.

When nine months' tide away had worn,
A son of that pure May is born,
As when we see a sunbeam pass
Vibrating through transparent glass;
As sunlight through whole glass finds way,
So of His mother shines, like ray,
This child, with her virginity
Left sealed in stainless purity.

34.

Such wonders never fell before,
That mother, yet a maiden, bore
Both man and God, and bade the same
The true salvation to proclaim:
The skies o'er wandering herdsmen sing
Their praises to the new born King.
The heavenly glory stoops on earth,
And men with angels praise his birth.

---

ljós = ljósi. It seems to be the poet's object to parallelize the twofold miracle: that a virgin-mother gave birth to a man-God (a God-man) to announce a new faith.—5-8. The order of this half-strophe and the following is inverted in A. These verses seem to be a free reproduction of the Latin:

'Gaudet chorus cœlestium,
Et angeli canunt deo,
Palamque fit pastoribus
Pastor creator omnium.'

B. R. 1629, p. 28–29.—6. Hirð-arar, A.—7. Himna dýrðin, B.

35.

Þó var ei svá rík, at reifa
Ríkust móðir ætti góða,
Því var konungr hörðu heyvi
Huldr, at hann mætti firrast kulda.
Umsníðíngar Jesú prýði
Atti dagr at fæðing váttar,
Œsist blóð á líkamann ljósan,
Lagast innileg tár à kinnum.

36.

A þrettánda dag til Drottins
Dýrðar menn, er ríkjum stýrðu
Austr í heim, með offrin komu,
Ungan mann at prísa á þann veg.
Umrennandi, sex at sinnum,
Sex daga grein, ok fjórum einum,
Offrast kaus fyrir oss at vísu
Jesús sjálfr í musteris hválfi.

35. 1-2. Þó var ei svá rík at reifum Rèttlát móðir er átti góðan. A. —3. Heyi, A.—4. At mætti hann, A.—5. Umsníðing á J., A.—6. Atta dag at fæðing, A.—7. Um lík., A.—8. Minnilig tár, B.

36. 1. Þrettánda, *i.e.* on the day of Epiphany, Jan. 6th, the thirteenth day after Yule.—

35.

Though full of might, the mother mild
Was yet too poor to swathe her child,
In hard straw she must needs enfold
The Lord, to keep him from the cold.
The eighth day from his birth was seen
His fair flesh circumcised, I ween;
The blood flows o'er his body weak,
And tender tears bedew his cheek.

36.

Unto the Lord the thirteenth day
Came chiefs endowed with kingly sway
In Eastern realms; rich offering
To honour that young man they bring;
A train of six times six days wore
Away with thereto added four,
When Jesus in the fane we find
Offered to God for all mankind.

3. Austan um heim, A.—4. Þeir heiðra þanninn, A.—5-6. This calculus of $6 \times 6 + 4 = 40$ days gives the festum purificationis V. Mariæ on the 2nd of February, forty days after Christmas, cpr. Levit. xii. 2, sqq.—6. Sjö daga gr., A.; ok fjórum einum, adopted from *Hist. Eccl.*; ok þar at einum, A.; þar til e., B.—7. Offrit kaus, A.

37.

Vígðist oss, þá er vatni dögðist,
Valdr himnanna, á þrítugs aldri,
I Jórdán með æðar hreinar;
Jón Baptista Drottni þjónar.
Þessi ástvin Jesú Kristí
Er nú váttr, er þann dag mátti
Samskínandi á grœnni grundu
Guðs þrenning með lýðum kennast.

38.

Finn ek, allt at mannvit manna
Mœðist, þegar er um skal rœða
Máttinn þinn, enn mikli Drottinn,
Meiri er hann, enn gjörvallt annat—

STEF.

Sè þèr dýrð með sannri prýði,
Súnginn heiðr af öllum túngum
Eilíflega, með sigri ok sælu,
Sœmd ok vald þitt minkist aldri.

---

37. 1, Er om. in A.—3. Við Jórdánar, A.—6. At þann d., A. —7. Sjá skínandi, B.

38. 2. Er om. in A.—3. Enn mildi, A.—4. Enn om. in B., no lacune left for it.—6-8. Left out in B.

37.

With water hallowed was the King
Of heaven by Jordan's crystal spring,
At thirty, fallen man to save;
John Baptist doth his Saviour lave:
This Jesus' well loved friend hath been
The witness, that that day was seen
On fair earth shining lovingly
'Mong men the holy Trinity.

38.

I feel how all man's wit grows weak
Attempting worthily to speak,
Lord, of thy power which doth, indeed,
All things existing far exceed—

STAVE.

Thine honour and thy bliss be sung,
Thy praise resound from every tongue,
Thy glory all triumphant be,
Thy power abide eternally.

39.

Undrast tók hinn forni fjandi
Fæddan mann, en skilja var bannat,
Og því líkt, sem andinn segði
Orðin slík af túngu forðum—
'Þykkir mèr, sem nýjung nokkur
Nálgist heim ok ættir beima,
Eitthvat klókt mun Drottinn dikta,
Duldr em ek, því at ferr af huldu.'

40.

'Jesúm tigna engla rásir
Upp ok niðr af himni þriðja,
Stjörnu-ljós ok fœrðar fórnir,
Friðar-samband á hverju landi;
Slík afla mèr sóttar-auka
Sönn stórmerkin veitt hjá mönnum,
Kvíði ek, at hans remming ráða
Ríði mèr at báðum síðum.

39. 2. En skilit var, A.—5. Þykki, B.—6. Eða ættir, B. 8. Duldr er ek, þat fer at, A.

40. 2. Uppi ok niðri í heimi þ., A.—7. Við hans r. r., A.

39.

The fiend to ponder much began
That maze, the birth of this new man,
And deemed as if to him of old
These words the Spirit had foretold—
'Methinks fresh wonders will befall
The orb of earth, and nations all;
The Lord doth plan some deep device
Hid from me under strange disguise.

40.

'All angels in the realms above
Bring Jesus their adoring love;
Him worship stars and offering hands
In bond of peace throughout all lands;
These signs, I see with sore dismay,
Shine forth to men in bright array;
From every side, I fear his rede
Will bring on me the direst need.

41.

'Föðr-ætt hans trúi ek fá munu hitta,
Finnst móðernit hèr með þjóðum,
Þó er atferðin Jesús burðar
Undarlig, svá at skil ek þat varla.
Ekki er mèr á þessum þokki,
Þann veg ferr þat únga manni;
Aldri var sá fyrr á foldu
Fœddur maðr er ek næsta hræddumst.'

42.

'Þyrstir hann, ok er fölr af föstum,
Firrist hlátr, en kann at gráta,
Mœðist hann, ok er móður sinnar
Mjólku fœddr, en reifum klæddur.
Finn ek þó, í slíku at sannast
Sjálf náttúran manndóm váttar,
Fýsir mik því fram at œsa
Flein ódygðar hánum at meini.'

41. 1. Faður ætt., B.; trúi ek fáir hitta, A.—4. At om. in A.—6. Þeim únga manni, A.; B's reading is here probably the more correct; manni, I take = menni, a diminutive of maðr, in a contemptuous sense, written with an *a* to satisfy the

41.

'His father's kin but few can trace,
His mother is of human race,
But his birth seems such mystery,
I wholly fail its mode to see;
This youngling's ways all thither wend,
That I can him no favours lend,
For none was born on earth afore,
Of whom such mighty dread I bore.

42.

'He thirsts, he fasts, his joys are brief,
He is acquainted well with grief;
He sucks a breast, and waxes tired,
And is in common swathe attired;
As thus I see that nature yet
Doth clearly forth his manhood set,
The goad of treason I am fain
To rouse in him to work his bane.

---

exigency of the metre.—8. Er om. in A.

42. 1. Þyrstr er h. ok fölr, A. —3. Hann ok á móður sinnar, A.—4. Mjólk uppfœddr, A.; klæddist, B.—5. At í slíku sannar, B.

43.

'Mèr virðist, sem miklu hærra
Mætur Guði hann Adam sæti,
Aðr ek sveik þau Evam bæði
Æru-snauð í písl ok dauða.
Satt er, at fæstir sjá við prettum,
Svá mun enn um Jesúm þenna;
Því treystumst ek framt at freista;
Forðum hefir ek slœgvitr orðit.'

44.

Sannur Máríu Sonrinn dŷri,
Sonur menniligr Guðs ok hennar,
Kenndu mèr, at forðast fjandann
Fjölkunnigan, en þèr at unna —

STEF.

Sè þèr dýrð með sannri prýði,
Súnginn heiðr af öllum túngum
Eilíflega, með sigri ok sælu,
Sœmd ok vald þitt minkist aldri.

---

43. 1. Sem miklu h., *Hist. Ecc.;* þat m. h., A.; hann miklu œðri, B.—2. Ef hann Adam s., B.—3. Evu, A.—8. F. hefi ek slœgur orðit, A.

43.

'Meseems that Adam sat of yore
Much higher with his God before
On him and Eve the curse I laid,
Which left them shamed to death betrayed;
In sooth my guiles are seen by few,
And so must fare this Jesus too,
To tempt him I will make full bold,
For I am crafty from of old.'

44.

True Son of Mary, Jesus good,
Incarnate Son of her and God,
Teach me to shun the subtle fiend,
And faithfully to be thy friend—

STAVE.

Thine honour and thy bliss be sung,
Thy praise resound from every tongue,
Thy glory all triumphant be,
Thy power abide eternally.

---

44. 1. Sonur M., A.—3. Kenn þú, A.—6. Only the three first words of the stave are given in B.

45.

Frètt hefir ek, at freistar Drottins
Föstu-móðs á ýmsum löstum
Púkans slœgð, er hvern mann hugði,
Hrekkjum vön, í synd at blekkja.
Vèla-kríngs á vöfðum strengjum
Vundin oft en snerust á lofti
Skeytin öll hin flærðarfullu
Fjandans brjóst í gegnum standa.

46.

Þessu næst hins kæra Kristí
Kenning tók um bygð at renna,
Líf-þjónanda lærisveina
Leitar, finnr, ok þar með veitir
Blindum, hrjúfum, dumbum, daufum
Dauðum, krömdum, œrum, lömdum,
Augu, grœðing, orð, at hlýða,
Andir, heilsu, vizku, at standa.

---

45. 2. Föstu meðr ok ýms., A. —3. Púkinn slœgr at hvern m., A.—4. Hvekkjum vanr, A.—5. At vöfnum str., A.—6. Vundust oft ok, A.—7. Hins flæðarfulla, A.—8. Fjanda brist, A.

46. 7. Augna grœðing orði at at hlýða, A.—8. Andar heilsu,

45.

The fiend essays in changing wise
The fasting Lord to tempt to vice,
For, guileful, every man he thought
To have in sin's defilement brought:
From strings wile woven hied full oft
His darts, but swerving turned aloft,
And, with his crafty forging fierce,
The fiend's own bosom they did pierce.

46.

The blessed Saviour's teaching now
Began throughout the land to flow,
Disciples he did search and save,
That life dispensing band, and gave
The blind, the weak, the crazed and lame,
The dead, bruised, deaf and dumb the same,
Their sight, and strength, and wit, and walk,
And breath, and health, and ear, and talk.

A.; although 'andir,' properly speaking, means 'souls,' I have translated the word as if it was sing. masc. 'anda,' 'breath,' that is to say, breath of life, which may be the original reading.

47.

Þetta sèr hann fjandi, at fættist
Fólkit hans; ok lízt þat vansi,
Dœmin góð at vaxa víða,
Verri brögð ok lýtin þverra.
Púkinn kvaldr ok þeigi þoldi
Þenna leik, er harðan kennir;
Því flýtandi sínum sveitum
Synda-brjót at drepa sem skjótast

48.

Leiðan dreng at ljótum ráðum
Lokkar hann svá, Jesús manna,
Yfir-morðinginn, innan hirðar,
Júdas nefndan, er óvænt stefndi:
Mildan Guð því að silfri seldi
Sveitum þeim er Júðar heita,
Fullum upp af grimdar galli,
Grenjaði þjóstr í þeirra brjósti.

---

47. 1. Fækkar, A.—3. Góð þau vaxa v., A.—4. En lýtin, B. —5. Kvaldur þeigi, A.—6. Er tók at kenna, A.; hafðan kennir, B.; I have here followed *Hist. Ecc.*—7. Sínar sveitir, B.

48. This strophe stands in a direct connexion with the preceding one, and the construction of the last two lines of strophe 47, taken together with the first half of the obscure

47.

This sees the fiend, how fewer grow
His folk, and deems it shameful how
All good examples growth will gain,
But vile deceit in turn doth wane;
The tortured fiend would not endure
This play, when he thereof was sure,
But urging on his bands to slay
This Sin-destroyer without delay

48.

The master-murderer does entice
Within the court to fell device
Lewd Judas, follower of the Lord,
Who, rushing now destruction ward,
The gracious Lord, most overbold,
To bands of Jews for silver sold,
Whose heart a galling rage did fill,
Whose breast did swell with evil will.

48th stanza, I take to be the following: 'Því flýtandi sínum sveitum at drepa sem skjótast syndabrjót lokkar yfirmorðinginn leiðan dreng Jesús manna, nefndan Júdas, að ljótum ráðum innan hirðar.—2. Lokkar hann þannin Jesú manninn, A.—4. Nefndan, so altered by the editor; Júdas nefndr, A., B., and the Edd.—5. Guð við silfri, A.—7. Fullur A.—8. Grenjandi, þ.

49.

Fúsir hlupu ok fundu Jesúm,
Fundinn hröktu, lömdu, ok bundu,
Bundinn leiddu, heiðnir hæddu,
Hæddan rœgðu, slógu, afklæddu.
Fjandans börn gjöra þröngvan þyrni,
Þessum spenna um blessat enni,
Þessir negldu Krist á krossinn,
Keyra járn, svá at stökk um dreyrinn.

50.

Ættim vèr á Jesúm Drottin
Ifunarlaust með fullu trausti
Ut af hjartans innstum rótum
Allir senn með gráti at kalla—

STEF.

Sè þèr dýrð með sannri prýði,
Súnginn heiðr af öllum túngum
Eilíflega, með sigri ok sælu,
Sœmd ok vald þitt minkist aldri.

---

49. 3. Hæðnir h., B.; heimskir h. A.—4. Slógu klæddan, B.; hæddan slógu ok afklæddu, A.—6. Þessir sp., B.; þenna sp., A.—7. Negla, A.—8. Svá stökk út dr. A.

49.

Now Jesus fain they searched and found,
And found they pushed him, struck and bound,
And bound they lead whom heathens mock,
Him mocked they smite, revile, unfrock;
These devils' sons twist piercing thorn
Around his blessed head for scorn,
And Christ they nail upon the rood,
From driven nails spouts forth the blood.

50.

O let us to our blessed Lord
A song in earnest faith accord,
From our hearts' depth let praises ring,
In tears let all devoutly sing —

STAVE.

Thine honour and thy bliss be sung,
Thy praise resound from every tongue,
Thy glory all triumphant be,
Thy power abide eternally.

50. 1 Ættum, A.—2. Efunarlaust, A.—5-8. See note to strophe 26; of the stef, B. gives only sè þèr dýrð með (af?).

51.

SIÐARI STEFJA-MÁL.

Yfirmeistarinn allra lista,
Jesús góðr, er lífgar þjóðir,
Kenn þú mèr, at stilla ok stýra,
Svá steflig orð megi túngan efla—

SIÐARA STEF.

Æfinlega með lyftum lófum
Lof rœðandi á hnè sín bæði
Skepnan öll er skyld at falla,
Skapari minn, fyrir ásjó þinni.

52.

Eru æ minnilig eftirdœmi
Yfirvaldanda himins ok landa:
Hneigði nú sinn háls, ok beygði
Hverjum þræl, er lysti at berja;
Fátalaðr, með lítillæti,
Lágraustaðr með ásján fagri,
Svá bjóðandi í sáran dauða
Sína önd fyrir nauðsyn mína.

51. See note to strophe 26.—4. Svá stefnlig, A.—7. Skyllþt (=skylt) at falli, A.—8. Asján, A.

51.

SECOND STAVE-LAY.

O Thou, who all good arts dost give,
Good Jesus, in whom nations live,
Teach me to rule and sway my tongue,
That fitly be this burthen sung—

SECOND STAVE.

With folded hands in loving way
Let all created beings say,
On kneeling knees in sweet accord,
Their praise before thy face, O Lord.

52.

O memorable example, now
The Lord of heaven and earth did bow
And bend his neck to the evil race
Of thralls who chose to smite his face:
Of few words, lowly in his mien,
And soft of speech, with face serene,
Himself to bitter death he gave,
That he my needy soul might save.

52. 1. Er æ, B.; eru minnil., A. —2. Yfirbjóðandi himins, A.— 3. Ok vægði.—6. Asján fagra, A. —7. I om. in B.; í sárum d , A.

53.

Hrækjandi mjök höfuðin skóku
Heiðíngjar, sem Júðar beiða,
Flestir allir flýðu Kristí
Fylgdar-menn við storminn þenna.
Minnast verð ek, má ei annat,
Móður Guðs, er í tárum flóði;
Mætti verða, at minna sótta
Minnast vildi hún eitthvert sinni.

54.

Höfut-drottningin, harmi þrúngin,
Hneigð ok lút, er skalf af sútum,
Fœrðist nær, þá er fèll úr sárum,
Fossum blóðit niðr á krossinn.
Þrútnar brjóst, en hjartat hristist,
Hold er klökt, en andinn snöktir,
Augun tóku at drukkna drjúgum,
Döpr ok móð í tára-flóði.

---

53. 1. Þá höfuð, A.—3. Kristum, A.—5. Ek ok má, A.—6. Móðir Guðs í vatni, A.—7. Verða minnar sóttar, A.—8. Vildir eitthv., A.

53.

The heathens by the Jews were led
To spit at Him, and wag their head,
And at this storm in fear and fright,
Most Jesus' followers took to flight;
I needs must tell how, rent with fears,
God's mother melted into tears,
That so some time it may befall
She will my sickness hard recall.

54.

The sorrow laden heavenly Queen,
Bent, trembling 'neath her grief, is seen
To draw anigh where fell, like foss,
From wounds the blood adown the cross:
Her breast doth swell, her heart doth sob,
Her flesh doth faint, her bosom throb,
Her weary eyes grow quickly dim,
As bathed in flood of tears they swim.

54. 3. Nær þar fèll, A.—4. Niðr um, A.—6. Holdit klökt en öndin snökti, A.—7. Drúkkna, A.

55.

Rödd engilsins kvennmann kvaddi,
Kvadda af engli Drottinn gladdi,
Gladdist mær þá frelsarann fœddi,
Fœddan sveininn reifum klœddi,
Klœddan með sèr löngum leiddi,
Leiddr à krossinn faðminn breiddi,
Breiddr à krossinn gumna grœddi,
Grœddi hann oss en helstríð mœddi.

56.

Þó grèt hún nú, sárra súta
Sverði níst í bringu ok herðar;
Sitt einbernit, sjálfan Drottin,
Sá hún hanganda á nöglum stangast;
Armar sviddu af brýndum broddum,
Brjóst er mœtt af þessum hætti,
Særðist bæði, Sonr ok Móðir
Sannheilög, fyrir grœðing manna.

55. 2. Kvaddan, A.—3. Þá frelsarann, A.—6. Leiddr af móður faðm, A.—8. Er helstríð, A.

56. 1. Sára súta, A.—5. Sviðu, A; sviddu, an irregularly formed past of svíða (sveið, sviðum,

55.

The angel voice, which erst addressed
The May, did her with joy invest,
With joy she bore the Saviour blest,
And her Son born in swathing dressed,
And dressed with her him ever led,
And led on cross his arms he spread,
Yea, spread them there in all men's stead,
And healed us all whereas he bled.

56.

Amid her tears the bitter sword
Of sorrow struck her, when the Lord,
Her only Son, on cross was hung,
Thereto with four sharp nails was stung:
From whetted spikes his arms do burn,
With agonies his breast is torn;
Through these dread sufferings must they go
The Holy Twain to heal our woe.

sviðu) in analogy with hlýða, níða, to suit the exigency of the metre (idd, odd).—6. Brjóstit mœtt, A.

57.

Fyrir Máríu faðminn dýra,
Fyrir Máríu grát enn sára,
Lát mik þinnar líknar njóta,
Lifandi Guð, með Syni ok Anda —

STEF.

Æfinlega með lyftum lófum
Lof rœðandi á knè sín bæði
Skepnan öll er skyld at falla,
Skapari minn, fyrir ásjó þinni.

58.

Syni Máríu svartir fœra
Seggir blandit gall með dreggjum;
Fulla smán ok flestar pínur
Fundu þeir, en heimrinn stundi.
Fölnar skinn, ok fellr at enni,
Fættust orð, en þurru mættir;
Andinn leið af Jesú píndum,
Yfirvaldanda himins ok landa.

---

57. 1. Maríu faðirinn dýri, A.—2. Grátinn sára, A.—4. Syni, so altered by the editor; föðr, A, B, and Edd.—5-8. See notes on 51, 5-8; of the stef B. gives only the first three words.

57.

Grant me, through Mary's bosom dear,
Through Mary's grief, and bitter tear,
Thy grace, for which I yearn the most,
O Father, Son, and Holy Ghost—

STAVE.

With folded hands in loving way
Let all created beings say,
On kneeling knees in sweet accord,
Their praise before thy face, O Lord.

58.

To Mary's Son the swarthy band
A cup of gall and eysel hand,
And o'er that woe and shame unknown
Upon him heaped the world must groan:
His visage sweet grows wan from pain,
His words grow few, his strength doth wane,
And Jesus, swaying the mighty host
Of heaven and earth, gave up the ghost.

58. 2. Blandat, A.—3. Fúla smán, A.—6. Fækka orð ok þverra m., A.—7. Ondin leið, A.

59.

Eg segi rètt, at enginn mætti
Ográtandi vörrum láta,
Jesú minn, ef letrið læsi,
Linhjartaðr, af pínu þinni;
Því at náttúran œpti af ótta
Öll skjálfandi, ok himnar sjálfir
Týndu ljós, þà er berr vart bundinn,
Bifaðist hauðr í þínum dauða.

60.

En í andláti Jesús sœta
Oss var flutt, at gægzt á krossinn
Fjandinn hafi, ok frètt at syndum,
Fœra-glöggr, ef nokkur væri.
Hlœgir mik, at hèr mun teygjast
Hans forvitni honum til vansa;
Eigi mun þá ormr hinn bjúgi
Agn-svelgjandi á krossi fagna.

59. 1. Ætti, A.—5. Nátt. ætti (œtti?), A.—7. Týndist ljós þá berr, A.

60. This strophe seems to be a reminiscence, or even a free treatment of the following discourse of St. Augustine on the words of the Saviour:

'"*Venit princeps mundi hujus, et in me nihil inveniet.*"—*Non ergo non invenit carnem, sed nihil suum, id est, nullum peccatum. Occidisti innocentem; peremisti quem non debebas, redde quod tenebas. Quid ergo ad horam exultasti, quia invenisti in Christo carnem mortalem? Muscipula tua erat: unde lætatus es, inde captus es. Ubi te exultasti aliquid invenisse, inde nunc doles quod possederas perdidisse.*' i.e., '"The prince of this world cometh, and hath nothing in me."—Therefore he found not only not the flesh, but nought of his own; that is, no sin. Thou hast killed the innocent; thou hast destroyed him whom thou

59.

I say aright, no man should hear
Without devotion most sincere
And smitten heart, the words that be
Recorded of Jesus' agony:
For nature cried from very fear,
All trembling, even the heavens clear
Did lose their light when thou wast bound,
In thy death quaked all earth around.

60.

But in sweet Jesus' death anigh
The cross, we hear, the fiend did spy,
If that, perchance, he might therein,
For ever watchful, find out sin:
But I rejoice that here he came
To have his fell greed put to shame;
For on the cross the worm enjoyed
Nowise the bait that him decoyed.

---

shouldst not have destroyed; give up what thou hast held. But what hadst thou to exult over that hour, in that thou foundest in Christ a mortal flesh? He was thy trap: by that, wherein thou rejoicedst, thou art taken prisoner. Whereas thou didst exult having found something, thou sorrowest now for having lost even that which thou possessedst.' St. Augustinus, Migne V. 745. Cpr.: '*Et quid fecit Redemptor noster captivatori nostro? Ad pretium nostrum tetendit muscipulam crucem suam, posuit ibi quasi escam sanguinem suum.*' i.e., 'And what did our Redeemer do to him who had taken us captives? For our ransom he tendered his cross as a trap wherein he put as a bait his own blood.' Ib. 726. Cpr. also '*Muscipula diaboli crux domini*;' i.e., 'the devil's trap, the cross of the Lord.' Ib. 1210.

2. Oss er fl. at gægðist, A.—3. Fjandinn hefði fr., A.—5. Forv. sèr at v., A.—8. A króki, B.

61.

Öll helvítis járnhlið skjálfa,
Undrast myrkr, er ljós er styrkra ;
Hlaupa fjandr, ok ætla undan,
Udœmin þeir sögðu at kœmi.
Hræðslan flaug um heljar bygðir,
Helga menn, er fjötrar spenna,
Hlaut óvinrinn laust at láta,
Lamdr ok meiddr, er valdit beiddi.

62.

Hvat er tíðinda ?—Hraktr er fjandinn.
Hverr vann sigrinn ?—Skaparinn manna.
Hvat er tíðinda ?—Helgir leiðast—
Hvert ?—Agæt í tignar sæti.
Hvat er tíðinda ?—Hjálpast lýðir.
Hví nú ?—Því lèt Jesús pínast.
Hvat er tíðinda ?—Himnar bjóðast—
Hverjum ?--Oss, vér prísum krossinn.

16.Cpr.'*Inferni claustra penetrans*
Tuos captivos redimens, &c.
Jesu nostra redemptio.
Horrens avernus infremit.'
Hymn B. R. 43.

'*Perrumpis infernum chaos,*
Victis catenas detrahis,
Victor triumpho nobili
Ad dexteram patris sedes.'
Hymn B. R. 44.—2. At ljós

61.

Now shake all iron gates of hell,
So light dismays the darkness fell;
The fiends appalled were fain of flight
From what they deemed a monstrous sight:
Pale dread through hell made speedy way,
The saints, who in hard fetters lay
Wounded and maimed, the fiend must hand
To freedom at the Power's command.

62.

What news?—The foe met hard defeat.
Who triumphed?—Man's Creator great.
What news?—The holy saints retreat—
Where?—To their blissful glory's seat.
What news?—The world is saved again.
How so?—Yea, e'en through Jesus' pain.
What news?—The heaven hath oped its door—
To whom now?—Us who the cross adore.

er, A.—3. Fjandar.—4. At om. in A.—8. Lamda ok meidda, A.

62. The order of the lines of this stanza is the following in A: 1-4=3-6, 5-6=1-2.—2. Sigur, A.—4. Agæt, so altered by the editor; hvert ágætir, B; hvert ágætt í, A.—6. Ok hví lèt nú J., A.—8. Oss er pr., A.

63.

Signað ljós, hinn sœti Jesús,
Sannur lífgari dauðra manna,
Drag þú mik frá djöfla-bygðum,
Drottinn blíðr, ok halt mèr síðan—

STEF.

Æfinlega með lyftum lófum
Lof rœðandi á knè sín bæði
Skepnan öll er skyld at falla,
Skapari minn, fyrir ásjó þinni.

64.

Sè ek ei þann, at út megi inna
Með orða snild, þó gjarna vildi,
Alla gleði, þá er fèkk at fullu
Forn Adám í Jesú kvámu.
Sjálfr hann at batt með bölvi
Börn sín öll í dauðans pínu,
En nú leysti oss öll úr banni
Eitt hans barn, er miskun veitti.

63. 1. Sign. lýsi enn, A.—2. Sanna lífgjöf, A.—5-8. See notes on strophe 51.—Of the stave only the first line is written in B.

63.

Sweet Jesus, O my blessed light,
Who dead men dost to life invite,
Drag me from out the devil's hold,
Dear Lord, and keep me in thy fold—

STAVE.

With folded hands in loving way
Let all created beings say,
Upon their knees in sweet accord,
Their praise before Thy face, O Lord.

64.

All skill of words would be in vain,
Though man endeavoured to explain,
What joy to Adam old it gave,
When Christ came, sinful man to save;
As he had bound with dreadful bale
His children all within death's pale,
Thus now released them from their ban
In mercy great the Son of Man.

64. 1. At om. in B.—2. Þó prófa v., A.—3. Þá om. in A.— 4. Við J. kv., A.; kvómu, B.— 7. Leysti öll, A.

65.

Hví stundaðir þú, hinn forni fjandi,
Fremdar-snauðr á Jesú dauða?
Eða þóttist þú meiri at mætti,
Máttrinn hans er guðdóm váttar?
Eður hugðir þú líkams lygðir,
At líkam tók hann meyjar ríkrar?
Overðugan hann flengdu fyrðar,
Flekklausan, hann er vann til ekki.

66.

Þú fyrirdœmdir auma Evam,
Eva mann, fyrir epli bannat,
Maðr bannsettur allar ættir,
Ættin Krist, er spjóti nisti;
Kristur þik, er fannt í fyrstu
Fyrstan prett, ok manndráp settir;
Svá ódygðar brandrinn bjúgi
Beygist aftr í þína kjafta.

---

65. 1. Því st., A.—2. A Kristí d., A.—3. Eður hugðist þ., A.—4. Máttrinn þinn enn guðdómr v., A.—5. Eður hugðist þú líkams lygði, A.—6. Líkama, A.—8. Flekklausastr vann til ekki, A.

66. This strophe is left meaningless in all MSS. and editions of 'Lilja.' The corruption of the text is brought about in such a curious way that an analysis of it is quite in place here. The commencing step is doubtless due to the anacoluthon of the verb *fyrirdæmdir*, which, when overlooked, was alone sufficient to make the stanza unintelligible to any scribe, and to give the impulse to all manner of attempts at rendering it rational. Collaterally with this went the corruption of the third line, due to a metrical difficulty. The word bannsettur, namely, has been used by the author, by way of license, as a trisyllable, but has undoubtedly been pronounced in the 14th century as a dissyllable, *bannsettr*, owing to theoverwhelming weight of the radical *sett* over the short and weak terminal *ur*. The same tendency makes itself manifest even in modern Icelandic pronunciation under similar circumstances. The termination *ur* instead of the older *r* was, besides, by no means so common in Eystein's lifetime, although great vacillation had crept into the language in that chapter of its grammar. When *bannsettur* was pronounced as a dissyllable the line became too short by one syllable, and did not scan. In filling up the gap, the vague idea that in the words

65.

Why didst thou, ancient fiend, desire
To see the Lord on rood expire?
Or deemedst thou to thee was given
A power above the Lord in heaven?
Didst thou as idle lying scorn
That Christ was of a virgin born?
Who, spotless, innocent, and pure,
Must now hard stripes of men endure.

66.

The poor Eve thou fordidst, and she
Her mate through one forbidden tree,
He cursèd, all his kin, they too
Their Christ, with spear him piercing through,
Thee Christ, for thou didst first device
The baneful murder and evil vice.
This rod of guile recoiling smote
Its hook thus in thy very throat.

'allar settir' there was implied a temporal notion, soon brought about the association of ideas with phrases like 'um allar aldir,' '*per omnia secula*,' and 'um aldr ok æfi,' '*per ætatem et ævum*,' and consequently the analogous and very plausible phrase 'um allar settir,' '*per omnes generationes*,' was coined. This done, the dislocation of the context was complete and the stanza left unintelligible. Dissolving the anacoluthon, the following is the construction of the stanza:—Þú (*i.e.* the devil) fyrirdœmdir auma Evu, Eva (fyrirdœmdi, 3rd pers. past. indic.) mann, ... maðr bannsettur (fyrirdœmdi) allar settir, settin (fyrirdœmdi) Krist, er spjóti nisti (hún hann), Kristr (fyrirdœmdi) þik, &c. I have kept the anacoluthon in the translation, but thereby, of course, rendered it exceedingly stiff—1. Evu, A.—2. Ok Evu mann, A.—3. Bannsettr um allar, A. B.—4. Ættin Krists er, A.; settin Krist á, B.; the *Hist. Ecc.* follows A. in the first couplet of this half strophe, but B. in the second.—5. Kristr af þèr at fann, A.; Kristr þik þó fann, *Hist. Ecc.*—6. Manndráps lystir, A.; á fyrstan prett ok manndráp þyrstan, *Hist. Ecc.*—7. Sá ódygðar broddrinn, A.—8 Beygðist, A.—The sense of the last couplet seems to be this: The chain of condemnation, which the poet calls the brand of the devil's guile, led from the first step, the betrayal of man, to the defeat of the devil himself in the death of Christ.

67.

Síðan reis með sigri af dauða
Sunnudag, ok gjörði kunnan
Sinn ódauðleik mörgum manni
Mildin sjálf, þó að deyja vildi.
Tvennar gengu tvisvar sinnum
Tíu dœgranna rásir hœgar,
Aðr en upp yfir himna hæðir
Hœfi' hann blóð, þat er tók af móður.

68.

Umrennandi svá at sinni
Sex daga grein ok fjórum einum,
Híngað sendi hann Heilagan Anda
Hreinferðugustum lærisveinum.
Vegsamligr til handar hœgri
Hann er Guðs, með virðing sannri,
Sinn bjóðandi faðm enn fríða
Fyrða laðar til himna dýrðar.

67. 3. Mörg. mönnum, A.—5-6. The calculus of this couplet refers to the forty days from Easter to Ascension Day.—8. Hóf þat blóð hann tók, A.

68. 1. Sex ath sínum, B.—2. Sjö daga g., A. The calculus

67.

Now from the dead triumphant rose
On Sunday morning, to disclose
To men his immortality
The gracious Lord, who chose to die.
A string of twice-told twenty days
Revolving passed their measured ways,
Before above the heavens high
The Lord ascended bodily.

68.

A train of six days passing wore
Away with thereto added four,
When hither he sent the Holy Ghost
To his disciples' righteous host;
And now he holds his kingly seat
On God's right hand, in glory meet;
With open arms he bids all come
To heaven, their true, their glorious home.

---

refers to the number of days between Ascension Day and Whitsunday, which is eleven (A) when both days are counted inclus., ten (B) if either is outtaken.—4. Hreinferðugastan, B. 6. Guð, A; sanna, A.—8. Fyrða at laða, A.

69.

Máríu son, fyrir miskun dýra,
Manns náttúru, ok líkam sannan,
Kennstu við, svà at mín þú minnist,
Mín, Drottinn, í ríki þínu—

STEF.

Æfinlega með lyftum lófum
Lof rœðandi á knè sín bæði
Skepnan öll er skyld at falla,
Skapari minn, fyrir ásjó þinni.

70.

Enn mun koma í öðru sinni
Allsvaldandi kungr, at gjalda
Seggjum verð fyrir sínar gjörðir,
Sóma-örr, á efsta dómi.
Svá geysar þá eldr ok eisa
Jörð ok fjöll, at í heimi öllum
Eigi finnst hèr upp úr skýjum
Obrunnit ok niðr at grunnum.

---

69. 2. Líkaman sanna, A.—3. Svá mætti minnast, A.—4. Minn, B.—5-8. See note on strophe 51; of the 'stef'

69.

Thee, Jesus, by thy mercy great,
Thy body and manhood, I entreat,
O, sweet Lord, to acknowledge me,
Me, in thy kingdom graciously—

STAVE.

With folded hands in loving way
Let all created beings say,
On kneeling knees in sweet accord,
Their praise before Thy face, O Lord.

70.

But to the earth shall come again
The mighty King, and to all men
From the last judgment's seat give forth
What all their deeds are truly worth ;
Then mead, and mount, and airy ways
In flames and embers stand ablaze,
From o'er the clouds is nothing found
Unburnt to down below the ground.

B. gives only the first two words.

70. 3. Seggia fyrðum s. gerðir, B.—6. Um jörð o. f. í heimi, A. —7. Hvergi finnst þá, A.

71.

Upprísöndum allra landa
Ibyggjurum við dóminn hryggva
Jesús munu þà sàrin sýnast
Sút-hrœrandi, ok píslar-fœri.
Orð ok hugsan, allar gjörðir
Eru kannaðar hvárs sem annars,
Bjóðast hvorki blót nè eiðar,
Byrgjast úti gjafir ok mútur.

72.

Enginn finnst á þessu þingi
Þrætu-gjarn með klókar varnir
Orða-hreims, er á Drottins dómi
Dreifast menn í flokka tvenna :
Aðra sveit með hæstum heiðri
Hefr hann langt yfir spheras efri;
Steypir þá, með eymd ok ópi,
Öðrum niðr í fjandann miðjan.

---

71. 1. Upprísundum, A.—2. Ibyggvir um d. B.—3. Jesús mun þá sárin sýna, A.—4. Ok Sin hrœrandi píslarf, A.—5. Orð

71.

When from their graves unto that doom
All nations rise in fear and gloom,
To them shall Christ his wounds unveil
And all his torture's woe and wail:
All words and thoughts, and every deed
Are searched of each and all; no heed
Is given to oaths or offerings,
All bribes are spurned and costly things.

72.

No one may quarrel, no one fall
To crafty strife or wordy brawl
At this assembly; wide apart
In twain hosts from it souls depart:
The one, in honour great and love,
God raiseth o'er the spheres above,
The other, with dread cries of woe,
He casts amid the fiends below.

hugsan, ok, A; gerðir, B.—6. Hvers ok ann., A.—8. Gáfur, A.

72. 2. Nè klókrar varnar, A. 3. Orða-hreimr á D., A.—7. En steypir, A; eymdar ópi, A.

73.

Reknir brott í dauðans drukknan
Drepnir menn, at þar skulu brenna,
Gnísta tennr í fýlu ok frosti,
Fjandr í kringum búka standa.
Brigzli ok hróp er at gjörðum glœpum,
Grimmleg sótt, í myrkri ok ótta,
Engin er vón á öðru en pínu,
Eilíf nauð, en kvikr er dauðinn.

74.

Þessu gegn munu finna fagnað
Fyrða hverr, til sinnar dýrðar
Sem Herrann bauð með hæstri prýði
Heim-leiðar, því at verða beimar
Ungir, glaðir, frjálsir, fríðir,
Fœrir, vitrir, máttkir, skærir;
Hátíð gild er um allar aldir
Alda þeim með virðing haldin.

73. 1. Drugknan, B; burt í dauðann dökkvan, A.—2. Er þar s., A.—3. I fjúki ok, A.—4. Sálir st., A.—5. Brigzl ok, A; glœpum gervum, B.

73.

Thus the doomed ones are chased aright
Into dire death and foulest plight,
Where teeth are gnashed, where chills the frost,
Where devils guard around the lost;
In scoffs and cries their deeds resound,
And gruesome plague and gloom abound;
For aught but plague, eternal pain,
And living death, all hope is vain.

74.

Against this shall have joyance sweet
All such, whom to their glory's seat
The Lord bids come triumphantly
Their homeward way; for then be they
All glad, and free, and fair, and young,
And hale, and wise, and bright, and strong;
They feast in honour meet and glee
Through ages everlastingly.

74. 1. Mun f. fögnut, A.—2. Fyrðum heim, B; til himna dýrð., A.—3. Sem herr. býðr, A.—4. Heimleiðir þær verða greiðar, A.—6. Maktir, A.—7. Er om. in A.—8. Alda þar er, A.

75.

Tárum rigni, en túngan þagni,
Taki af mál, en þurftug sálin
Berìst um fast, svá at búkinn hristi,
Bið ek óttandi, hjálp mèr, Dróttinn.

STEF.

Æfinlega með lyftum lófum
Lof rœðandi á knè sín bæði
Skepnan öll er skyld at falla,
Skapari minn, fyrir ásjó þinni.

76.

Tvá hræðumst ek, dóm ok dauða;
Deyr sá margr, er enginn bjargar;
Mitt eitt veit ek líf hit ljóta
Leiða mik í Drottins reiði.
Af margfaldri synda saurgan
Svíður brjóst, ok hefndum kvíðir
Fyrir afbrigði flestra dygða,
Fátt er þat er siðuna vátti.

---

75. 1. Túngan þagni en tárin rigni, A.—2. Tekr af m., A.—3. Berst um f. en búkrinn hristist, A.—5-8. See note to

75.

O tears, pour down, O tongue, be still,
O speech, grow hushed, my soul and will,
Strive hard, in trembling heart I cry,
And pray in fear, Lord, help thou me.

STAVE.

With folded hands in loving way
Let all created beings say,
On kneeling knees in sweet accord,
Their praise before thy face, O Lord.

76.

Of death and doom full fear I have,
How many die, whom none may save ;
My sinful life, I wot, indeed,
Must me into God's anger lead ;
My breast, by sin defiled, is rent
With dread of future punishment,
For in most things I do transgress,
In few I show my righteousness.

---

strophe 51; of the stef only the first line is written in B.

76. 2. At enginn, A.—3. Lífit, A.—5. Ok margf., A.—8. Fátt er gott er siðina vottar, A.

77.

Vindi fullt hefir veslan anda
Várn ofbeldit löngum hreldan,
Blár ok ljótr í öfundar eitri
Jafnan hefi ek næsta kafnat.
Reiði-gall með sárum sullum
Sviðrar mèr um blásin iðrin;
Hrygðin slítr af hjarta-rótum
Harðan styrk í súta myrkri.

78.

Festist ok með fjúki lasta
Fróst ágirndar mèr í brjósti,
Græðgi drep með glœpum auðgum
Grefst hèr inn með krókum stinnum.
Hræðilega með blindri blíðu
Blekkist hold af dauðans flekkun.
Heldr af slíku ætti ek aldri
Ugglaus vera, þó að miskun huggi.

77. 2. Obbelldith, B; vort ofbeldit, A.—7. Hrygð slítur af h., A.

78. 1. Fest. oft í f., A.—3. Græðgin drepr með, A.—6. Flekkum, B.

77.

Inflated passions, past control,
How often do they grieve my soul,
With envy's poison stifled, too,
How loathsome was I oft and blue;
The gall of wrath through ulcers sore
Doth scorch my bowels to the core;
'Mid sorrows' gloom regretful wail
My whole heart's manful strength doth quail.

78.

Full oft in storms of guilt and vice
My breast doth freeze with avarice;
And deadly greed, abounding crime,
Their sting will bury there many a time;
My flesh blind pleasures sweetly guile,
Yea and with deadly things defile;
Then let me never heedless be,
Though, Christ, thy mercy comfort me.

79.

Fyrirláti mèr Faðir hinn sœti,
Fyrirláti mèr, ek vil gráta
Orð ok hugsan, allar gjörðir,
Auðmjúklegast, ok firrast dauða;
Því lýt ek nú þèr at fótum,
Þrangdr ok kvaldr af mœðing taldri;
Klökkur, hræddr, ek þurfa þykkjumst
Þína vægð í nauðum mínum.

80.

Svá fýsumst ek, hinn sœti Jesú,
Synda-líkn, at þeirra myndir
Lítast mèr sem liggi þrútit
Linna eitr um hjartat innan.
Send híngað mèr Sjöfalds Anda
Sanna gift, er leysi úr banni
Mína önd, svá at mættag þjóna,
Maríu Blóm, fyrir yðarn sóma.

79. 1. Faðirinn s., A.—3. Illar gjörd., A.—4. Auðmjúklega ok firrast dauðann, A.—6. Þreyngdr, A.; þraungdr, *Hist. Ecc.* (þrangdr = þrengdr, *Dan.* trang).

79.

O Father sweet, forgive thou me,
Forgive me, rueing earnestly
All thoughts, and words, and every deed
That from death's power I may be freed;
I sink down to thy feet for rest,
With my affliction hard oppressed;
Afeard and humble I implore
Thy mercy in my need so sore.

80.

My sins' forgiveness I desire,
O Lord, for in their nature dire,
They seem like serpents' poison fell,
That rank within the heart doth swell;
Oh, send thou hitherward to me
The Sevenfold Spirit's grace, to free
My curse bound soul, that serve I may,
O Mary's Bloom, thy majesty.

---

7. Klökkr ok hr., A.—8. I nauðsyn mínum, A.
80. 1. Enn sœti Jesus, A.— 2. Að þuera my[n]di, B.— 6. Gift svá leysi, A.—7. At om. in A.—8. Blómi yðvarñ, A.

81.

Laust aldrigi þú lát mik, Kristi,
Lasta-vinds í bylja-kasti;
Typta mitt ok tem sem oftast
Tendrat brjóst með líknar vendi;
Svá at grátandi ok fúss at fótum,
Faðir skínandi, krjúpa ek þínum,
I hvert þat sinn, er ek kulda kenni
I kostalausu glœpa-frosti.

82.

Beiði ek nú fyrir Maríu Móður
Mjúka bœn ok fagran tænað,
A treystandi, Jesú Kristi,
Yðra vægð, er týndum nœgðist:
Pín mik, áðr enn detti á dauði,
Dróttinn minn, í kvölum ok sóttum,
At því miður sè ek þá síðan
Slitinn á fjandans króki bitrum.

---

81. 1. Þú om. in A.—3. Typta mik, A.—5. Krjúpi ek, A.— 6. Er om. in A; kuldans, A.— 8. Af kostal, A.

81.

Leave me, Christ, ne'er astray to go
Where vice's blighting whirlwinds blow.
Chastise, correct my heart, O God,
Enkindled by thy mercy's rod;
That fain of heart, though sore I weep,
O Father, to thy feet I creep,
Whene'er on me is laid a hold
By deadly sin's benumbing cold.

82.

By Mary Mother I entreat,
By her prayer and favour sweet,
A-trusting Jesus' sacrifice,
Which for a lost world did suffice:
Try me, O Lord, with plague and pain,
Ere I by sudden death be slain;
That by the devil's crook I be
The less torn in eternity.

---

82. 1-2. Beiði ek þik nú, mær ok móðir, Fyrir mjúka ást ok dygðir skástar. A. —4. Yðar vægð, A.—5. Dettr á, A.—6. Dr. ótt í, A.—7. Því mnnir, B.

83.

Lífið sjálft, að lúktri æfi
Leys mitt bann fyrir iðran sanna;
Oleu-smurðr ek vænti at ek verða,
Viðurkennandi mjúkleik þenna.
Hreinast gef þú hjarta mínu
Hold ok blóð, þat er tókt af móður,
Listuligu að leiðar nesti,
Þá leysist önd af holdsins böndum.

84.

Hræðumst ek, at sárt muni svíða
Samvizkunnar bygð af grunnum,
Sundruð öll, þá er syndir kalla
Sína eign á hjarta mínu.
Dökkvir munu þá fjandans flokkar
Fœrast að með ópi ok kæru,
Búnir mik at brenna ok skeina,
Bíta, kremja, rífa ok slíta.

83. 3. Smurðr ath ek uænti ath ek uerða, B, veittu at ek, A. —4. Fögnut þenna, A.—6. Bl. er tókst af móðr, A.—7. Listuligha, B.; listugasta leiðarn, A.—8. Þá added agreeably to *Hist. Ecc.*

83.

Grant me, repentant, sweet repose
From my hard ban, when life doth close;
Grant the last ointment I receive
While yet its grace I may conceive;
Grant thou unto my dying heart
Of thy pure body and blood a part,
Sweet lode-fare to my soul, when free
From fleshly bonds it soars to thee.

84.

My conscience-home, mefears, will sore
Be burnt down to its very core
In sunder torn, when sin shall call
For what it owes in my heart withal;
And fiends in swarthy bands draw nigh
With accusation's yelling cry,
Ready to burn, and wound, and maim,
And tear, and rack, and rive my frame.

84. 1. Munn, B.—2. Af grunni, A.—3. Syndrast ö., A. —4. I hjarta m., A.—6. Fœr. nær, A.—7. Ok pína, A.

85.

Muntu þetta, enn dýri Drottinn,
Djöfla-sveitum nöktum veita,
Mína önd at meiða ok skeina,
Maríu-barn, en hjálpar varna?
Með heitu ok rauðu hjartans blóði
Hana leystir, ok því má ek treysta,
Jesú, þinni ást, er mönnum
Öllum bauð til lífs frá dauða.

86.

Heyrðu mik nú, himins ok jarðar
Háleit bygðin allra dygða,
Meyja, drottningin manna ok engla,
Móðir Guðs, ok lœkning þjóða:
Þá er mœðumst í nógum nauðum,
Nálæg vertu minni sálu,
Vefðu ágætu verndar skauti,
Von mín sönn, til hjálpar mönnum.

85. 2. Nokkut, A, *Hist. Eccl.* —3. Ok pína, A.—4. Hjálpar, A. —5. Hjarta-blóði, A.—6. Hana leysti þú, því vil ek treysta, A. —7. Er ed. alteration; ok, B; Jesús sínum ástarmönnum, A.

86. 2. Háleit frig*in, A.—3. Cpr. *Virgo Maria, regina angelorum, domina mundi, B. R. Officia Sanctorum;* megin-drottningin, B.—5-8. Cpr. '*Sub tuum præsidium confugimus, sancta dei genitrix, nostras deprecationes ne despicias in necessitatibus nostris,*

85.

O sweet Lord, Mary's child, wilt thou
These naked devils' hosts allow
My soul with tortures dire to try,
Or to me, weak, thine help deny?
Nay, by thy warm red heart's blood thou
Hast ransomed it, I trust and trow;
For thou thy well belovèd all
From death to lasting life didst call.

86.

Deign thou, adorned with virtues dear
In heaven and earth, my prayer to hear,
O Queen of men and angels, Maid,
O Mother of God, all nations aid:
When with hard need exceedingly
My soul is tried, be nigh to me;
Our aid, in thee our hope we have,
With thy protecting arm us save.

---

sed a periculis cunctis libera nos semper, virgo benedicta! quia tu es spes unica peccatorum.' i.e. 'We flee for refuge under thy protection, O holy Mother of God; despise not our prayers in our need, but deliver us from all dangers for ever, O blessed Virgin, for thou art the sinner's only hope.' *Brev. Rom.*, 1551, 578.—5. Þá ek m., A.—6. Nálægri vertu, A.—8. Sönn, þú hj., A.

87.

Maria, kreistu mjólk úr brjóstum,
Mín drottning, fyrir barni þínu;
Dreyrug föðrnum sýndu sárin,
Son Máríu, er naglar skáru;
Ek vænumst at ykkrum þjóni
Engin kvöl megi drottna lengi,
Miskunnar þá er mjúkust renna
Merkin slík um himnaríki.

88.

Frammi stattu, er fœddir Drottin,
Fyrir skínanda barni þínu,
Miskun, bið þú, at mjúka finni
Maðrinn hverr, en glœpir þverri;
Berðu enn fram með blíðum vörum
Bœnar-mál fyrir kristnum sálum,
María, Jesú móðir dýrust,
Mundu, at eigi skiljumst ek undan.

---

87. 1. Kreist þú, A.—3. Sýn þú, A.—4. Sonur, A.
88. Cpr. '*Monstra te esse matrem,*
Sumat per te preces,
Qui pro nobis natus,
(Tulit esse tuus).
Virgo singularis,
Inter omnes mitis,

87.

Press milk from breast, O Mary mild,
My Queen, before thy very child;
Thy deep wounds show thy Father dear,
O Mary's Son, whom nails did tear;
Then trust I no tormenting pain
Your servant needs must long sustain;
If these sweet signs of mercy be
Shown forth on high on behalf of me.

88.

O thou, Lord Jesus' mother sweet,
Stand forth, thy radiant child entreat,
That grace abundant be the gain
Of all, but sin and guilt may wane;
Give forth from out thy lips most sweet
For Christian souls thy prayers well meet,
Dear Jesus' mother, mind thou me,
That I may not forgotten be.

Nos, culpis solutos,
Mites fac et castos.'
—1. Statt þú, A.—2. Skínandi b. A.—3. Mikla finni, A.; finnir, B.—5. Ber þú fram af b., A.—6.—Kristnar sálir.

89.

Þú ert hreinlífis dygðar dúfa,
Dóttir Guðs, ok lækning sótta,
Giftu-vegr, ok geisli lofta,
Gimsteinn brúða, ok drottning himna,
Guðs herbergi, ok gleyming sorga,
Gleðinnar past, ok eyðing lasta,
Líknar-æðr, ok lífgan þjóða,
Loflig mær, þú ert englum hærri.

90.

Þú ert hitnandi Heilags Anda
Höll, ok prýdd með dáðum öllum,
Ei kennandi kvitt af syndum,
Krafta þröng, nè löstinn öngvan.
Þú ert elskan ein af sprundum,
Agætust fyrir lítillæti.
Umbœtandi bragna syndir,
Blessut Mær, þú ert Drottni kærust.

89 = 90 in *Hist. Eccl.*—1. Hrein lífiss, B.; dygðug, A.—3. Cpr. Mulier amicta sole.—4. En drottn., A.—5. Ok om. in A.

90 = 89 in *Hist. Eccl.*—1-4 comes last in B, but A.'s arrangement seems to be, on the whole, a better one,—2. Hölld (= höll), B; höllin, A.—3.

89.

Thou'rt dove of pure and virtuous life,
And daughter of God, and leech for strife,
The way of bliss, ethereal sheen,
And gem of mays, and heaven's Queen;
God's harbour, grief's oblivion's well,
Delight of joy, who sin dost quell,
Compassion's vein, and nations' aid,
Above all angels honoured Maid.

90.

Thou'rt the warm Holy Spirit's hall,
Bedecked with deeds right glorious all;
No trace thou knowest of unright
Or guilt, or yet of want of might;
'Mong women thee alone we bless
And love thee for thine humbleness;
For pity on sinners thou dost pray,
Most loved of God, O blessed May.

'Kvitt' I take here to mean 'an inkling,' 'aught,' a signification which the word has still in the east of Iceland, in conventional use.—4. Nè, ed-alteration; en A, B, and *Hist. Eccl.*—5. Elskandi ein A, *Hist. Eccl.*—8. Þú ert englum hærri, A, *Hist. Eccl.*

91.

Máría, ertu móðir dýrust,
Máría, lifirðu sœmd í hári,
Máría, ertu af miskun skærust,
Máría, lèttu synda-fárit;
Máría, lýtin mörg því vóru,
Máría, líttu klökk á tárin,
Máría, grœð þú mein hin stóru,
Máría, dreif þú smyrsl í sárin.

92.

Túngu-sœtr ef einnhverr ýta
Orðum hyggst í kvæði at skorða
Mjúkan dikt, at maklegleikum,
Mín drottning, af heiðri þínum:
Því er líkast, sem rasi ok reiki
Ráðlauss seggr at ýmsum veggjum,
Fældr ok byrgðr, ok feti þó hvergi,
Fús í burt úr völundar húsi.

91. 1. Móðir skærust, A.—2. Hári = hárri; lofa þú sœtu ári, A. — 3. Kærust, B. — 4. Leittu, B.—5. M. lít þau mein er vóru, A.—6. Lít þú, A.—7. Meinin, A.—8. Ber þú, A.

92. Cpr. *Quas tibi laudes fragilitas humani generis persolvat,*

91.

Thou, Mary, art our mother bright,
Thou, Mary, art with honour dight,
Thou, Mary, beamest bright with love,
O Mary, baleful sin remove;
O Mary, by our faults and fears,
O Mary, heed our flowing tears,
O Mary, our great afflictions calm,
Pour, Mary, o'er our wounds thy balm.

92

Who so o' the sweetliest speaking tongue
Should try with words to fit in song
What praise there could be meetly said
To honour thee, O Queen, O Maid,
He'd liken one, who wildered all
Goes stumbling on 'twixt wall and wall,
And scarred, hemmed round, can find no way
From out the maze to gain the day.

quæ solo tuo commercio recuperandi aditum invenit?' B. R. 1551, fol. 578.—1. Tungan sœtur einhv., A.—2. Orðin, A.—7. Birðr, A.—8. Fúss, B, A. I have followed the modern spelling fús in order to meet the exigency of the rhyme.

93.

Hrœrð af list þó að hvers manns yrði
Hold ok bein at túngum einum,
Vindur, leiptr ok grœnar grundir,
Grös ilmandi, duft ok sandar,
Hagl ok drif, sem fjaðrir fugla,
Fiskar, dýr, sem holt ok mýrar,
Hár ok korn, sem heiðar stjörnur,
Hreistur, ull, sem dropar ok gneistar,

94.

Viðr ok grjót, sem staðir ok stræti,
Strengr himnanna, loft ok englar,
Orma-sveit ok akrar hvítir,
Iturr málmr, sem laufit pálma:
Augnabragð þótt aldri þegði,
Allar þær af fyrnsku væri
Móðar, fyrr en Maríu prýði
Mætti skýra fullum hætti.

93. This and the following stanza form an anacoluthon, whereas the opening sentence: 'Hrœrð þó at yrði at túngum einum,' applies to all the things enumerated from 93, 2–94, 4.—1. Om. in A.—2. Af túng, A.—3. Lept[7] (=leptur) grœnar, B.—8. Hreistr ok ull, A; neistar, A.

93.

Let change e'en into tongues alone
Of every man his flesh and bone,
And winds and lightnings, green-clad land,
And fragrant herbs, and dust and sand,
And hail, and feathered fowl, and snow,
And fish, and hills, and marshes low,
And hair, and twinkling stars, and grain,
And scaled things, wool, and sparks, and rain,

94.

And woods, and stones, and cities fair,
And angels, heavenly chords, and air,
And worm-hosts, fields with harvest white,
And palm-woods tall, and metals bright:
Though not one while their peace they held,
Yet must they wane away to eld,
Or e'er they fittingly had said
Thy honour's praises, Mary Maid.

94. 1. Viðir, A; sem steinar, B.—2. Strengir himna, A.—3. Sem akrar, A.—4. Jurtir málmur, B; ok lauf., A.—5. Augna-brögð, A.—6. Ok andir þær, A.—7. Máðar, B.—I have preferred A.'s reading, because it seems clearly to point to the classical reminiscence elli-móðr, decrepid.—8. Skýrast, A.

95.

María, vertu mèr í hjarta,
Mildin sjálf, því at gjarna vildak,
Blessut, þèr, ef mætta ek meira,
Margfaldaðan lofsöng gjalda.
Loflig orð í ljóða-gjörðum
Lystuligrar móður Kristi,
Engum tjóar at auka lengra:
Einn er Drottinn Maríu hreinni.

96.

Enn krossfesti kraftrinn hæsti,
Kristr, er fjórir broddar nistu,
Þèr býð ek ok þinni móður
Þetta verk, er í einn stað setteg.
Þá látit mik þessa njóta
Þröngskorðaðra kvæðis orða,
At þit sjáit mik öllu varða,
Öndin mín at forðist pínu.

95. 1. Ertu, A.—2. Því ek gjarnan vildi, A.—3. Ef ek mætta meira.—4. Þèr repeated after margfaldaðan in A.—5. Líflig, B.—6. Listul., B; Listuligri, A.—7. Tjáir, A.

95.

With loving kindness, Mary, deign
My heart to fill, as I would fain,
That, if I might still farther bring
My lay, thy praise therein should ring;
But higher praise, in verses made
On Christ's dear Mother could ne'er be said,
Than that thou art by God alone,
O May, in purity outshone.

96.

Thou, highest power, who nailed on rood
With four spikes, there didst shed thy blood,
To thee, and to thy Mother bright,
This my own work I now indite;
O, let this close and rigid rhyme
Avail me at that very time,
Whenas ye know that all my need
Is, that my soul from pain be freed.

---

96. 1. Þú enn, A.—2. Nistu dropped without a lacune in B. —4. Þetta verk er ek í einn stað setti, A.—5. Þessarra, A, *Hist. Eccl.*—6. Er þit sjáit, A.

97.

Veri kátar nú, virða sveitir.—
Vætti ek þess, í kvæðis hætti
Varkunnigr, at verka þenna
Vanda ek minnr en þætti standa.
Varðar mest, at allra orða
Undirstaðan sè rèttlig fundin,
Eigi glögg þó Eddu regla
Undan hljóti at víkja stundum.

98.

Sá er óðinn skal vandan velja,
Velr svá mörg í kvœði at fela
Hulin fornyrðin, trautt má telja,
Tel ek þenna svá skilning dvelja.
Vel því at hèr má skír orð skilja,
Skili þjóðir minn ljósan vilja:
Tal úbreytiligt veit at vilja;
Vil at drápan heiti Lilja.

97. 1. Verit, A.—2. Ek om. in B; vænti ek þess., A.—3-4. Vorkinnit mèr verknat þenna þó vandi ek miðr en þykki til standa, A; þèr varkynnit, þótt verka þenna vanda ek miðr en þykki til standa, *Hist. Eccl.*—5. Þat varð. m. til all., A.—6. Rèttilig.—8. For hljóti, which I have adopted from *Hist. Eccl.*;

97.

Good folk, be now of merry cheer.—
For want of metric skill I fear
My song is writ, as some may deem,
Less meetly than befits its theme;
Thereon lieth most, the certain ground
Of every word be clearly found,
With Edda's rules, obscure in thought,
When needful, being set at nought.

98.

He who doth choose artistic song
Must hide within his verse a throng
Of olden spells without an end
Which make songs hard to comprehend;
But my plain words may all conceive,
Good people, here my will perceive:
That artless speech was all my aim;
Let LILY be the poem's name.

A and B read verði, which is inadmissible on prosodical grounds.

98. 1. Vanda ok, A.—2. Velr margt í kvædi at fela, A.—4. Til ek þau megi sk., A.—5. At om. in A.—6. Tal óbreytt er veitt af vilja, A.—8. At om. in A et B.

99.

Sannri ást af sœtu brjósti,
Sinni, rètt, fyrir hjálp ok minni,
Segi Maríu, hverr er heyrir,
Hennar vess á diktan þessa.
Vera kann þá, at mærin minnist
Mín, þá er liggur kvaldr í pínu.
Berr mik þar til ván, á vörrum
Víst ef lèki: Dominus tecum.

100.

Almáttigr Guð allrar stettar,
Yfir-bjóðandinn engla ok þjóða,
Ei þurfandi staða nè stunda,
Stað haldandi í kyrrleiks valdi;
Senn verandi úti ok inni,
Uppi ok niðri, ok þar í miðju,
Lof sè þèr, um aldr ok æfi,
Eining sönn í þrennum greinum.

---

99. 1-2. I have translated hjálp ok minni as referring to a correct recital of Eystein's song. Older translations render hjálp as salvation, and turn the line thus, 'for his and for mine salvation;' but the word rètt seems to me to point the other way.—

99.

With loving heart, devoutedly,
By help and by your memory,
Ye all unto your Mary say
Aright her verse in this my lay;
Mayhap, then will the Maiden deign
To mind me, when brought low with pain;
A-trusting this be granted me
I sing: the good Lord be with thee.

100.

Almighty God of every state,
Who angels rulest, and nations fate,
Who needest neither place nor hour,
Abiding in thy tranquil power,
At once abroad, and yet within,
Above, below, and there between;
Through ages everlastingly
Be praised, O one in Trinity.

1. Af sannri á. ok s., A.—2. Reitt, B.—4. Vers ok, A; by this line ends 'The Lily' in A.—6. Leki, A B and Edd.—The song ends in 'Berg's Book' with Dom. tecum.

GLOSSARY.

á, prep. with dat, and acc. *in, on, over, of*; von á himna sælu *hope of heaven's bliss.*
á, *see* eiga.
áðr, adv. temp. *formerly, before; á.* enn *ere, before.*
af, prep. *of, from, by.* 1, local—*motus ex loco:* reis af dauða *rose from the dead;* dreyri af síðu-sári *blood from a wound in the side;* öndin leið af Jesú *the spirit departed from.* 2, disjunctive—*from:* hrygð slítr af hjarta-rótum *tears from the heart's roots.* 3, partitive—*of, from among:* þú ert elskandi ein af sprundum *alone among women.* 4, subjective—*by:* kvadda af engli, &c. *addressed by the angel.* 5, objective—*of, about:* súngu af sínum kungum *sang of or about their kings.* 6, causal—*a,* concrete, *from, by, with:* armar sviddu af brýndum broddum *from whetted spikes;* slitinn af fjandans króki, *torn by the fiend's hook. b,* abstract—*through, by:* hrœrð af list *moved through art;* af mœðing taldri, *from the said agony.* 7, emotional—*from, with:* œpti af ótta *cried from or with fear.*
afbrigði, n. pl. *deviation, trespass.*
afklæða (-dda, -tt), v.a. *to unclothe, unfrock, strip.*
afla (-aða, -at.), v. a. *to procure, provide, cause.*
afsprengr (-s,–), m. *offspring.*
afsprengi (-is,–), n. id.
ágirni, f. indecl. *covetousness, greed.*
agn-svelgjandi, pa. *bait-swallowing.*
ágætr, ad. *excellent, glorious.*
akr (-s, -rar), m. (*acre*), *field.*
alda, gen. pl. *see* öld.
aldin (-s, id), n. *fruit.*
aldin-skógr, m. *fruit-forest, fruit-bearing wood.*
aldri, aldrei, aldrigi (from aldr *age,* and eigi, gi, negative particles, = *not in age*), adv. *never.*
allr (öll, allt; gen. alls, allrar, alls; dat. öllum, allri, öllu; acc. allan, alla, allt; pl. nom. allir, allar, öll; gen. allra; dat. öllum; acc. alla, allar, öll), ad. *all.*
almáttigr, ad. *almighty.*
allsvaldandi, pa. id.
anda-gift (-ar, -ir), f. *spiritual gift, vision.*
andar, *see* önd.
andi (-a, -ar), m. *spirit, ghost; Holy Ghost.*
andlát (-s, id), n. *demise, death.*
andlit (-s, id), n. *a countenance.*
andlits-hvítr, ad. *bright-faced, fair-faced.*
andvani (vani = Engl. *wane*), ad., *void of life; expers.*
annarr (önnur, annat; gen. annars, annarrar, annars; dat. öðrum, annarri, öðru; acc. annan, aðra, annat; pl. nom. aðrir, aðrar, önnur; gen. annarra; dat. öðrum; acc. aðra, aðrar, önnur), ad. *other, second;* flest allt annat *most things else.*
ár (-s, id), n. *a year.*
armr (-s, ar), m. *an arm.*

ásján (-ar, -ir), f. *face, countenance.*
ásjó, f. id.
ást (-ar, -ir), f. *love, affection.*
ástar-menn, *beloved people.*
ástvin, m. *beloved friend.*
at (1), *nota infinitivi, to;* at spillast *to become corrupt.*
at (2), conj. with ind. subj. and infinit. *that, to, in order to.* 1, with ind. of facts real or presumed as real: at líkama tók hann *that he assumed flesh;* at fæstir sjá við prettum *that few indeed heed guiles;* at freistar Drottins; undrast myrkr at ljós er styrkra. 2, with subj. very frequent: at renni mál *that speech may flow;* at mætti orðin *that the words might,* &c. 3, with infin. *a, to:* skyldr at fœra *bound to bring;* in this sense it is often dropped: bjóða mèr í frásögn fœra (= at f.) *bid me to relate.* *b, in order to:* enn mun koma at gjalda *in order to pay;* fyrða at laða *for the purpose of inviting people.*
at (3), pron. relat. = er: fyrri menn at frœðin kunnu *who knew;* púkinn slœgr at hvern mann hugði *who had the mind to.*
at (4), prep. with dat. and acc. *after, to.* 1, with acc. *after:* átti dagr at fœðing *the eighth day after the birth.* 2, with dat.—*a,* local (*motus ad locum*) *to, towards:* at fótum *towards the feet;* at báðum siðum *towards, into both sides;* abstract: at ljótum ráðum *into evil counsel;* at vansa, *into* shame.—*b,* with a primary idea of motion: at lesti *after, following sin.*—*c,* with a primary temporal notion *after, in consequence of, by:* at rèttum dómi, *by a just doom.*—*d, about:* frètta at syndum *to enquire about sins.* *e, in comparison to:* at makleg-leikum *pro meritis.*—*f,* with a past part. at forms a grammatical figure similar to *ablativus absolutus* in Latin: at höldnu innsigli *the seal being holden or preserved.*—*g,* with neuters of adjectives it forms an adverbial notion: at huldu *clandestinely,* at vísu *certainly,* at fullu *fully,* &c.
át, 1 and 3, past ind. of eta.
atferð, f. *manner, mode of taking place.*
áttboge (átt *family,* bogi *a bow*), m. *a generation.*
átti, 1 and 3. past ind. of eiga.
átti (= áttundi), num. ord. *the eighth.*
attú = at þú *that thou.*
áttu = átt þú, 2, pres. imperat. of eiga.
auðginntr, ad. *easily tempted, simple.*
auðgr (contr. for auðigr), ad. *plentiful.*
auðmjúklega, adv. *humbly.*
auga (id, -u), n. *an eye.*
augabragð, n. *twinkle of an eye.*
augnabragð, id.
augna-grœðing, f. *eye-healing.*
augsjón, f. *eye-sight.*
auka (eyk, jók, jukum, yki, aukit), v. a. *to eke out.*
aumr, ad. *wretched.*
austan (orig. a weak noun), adv. *from, through the east.*
austr. (-s,–), n. *the east;* a. í heim *east in the world.*
ave, lat. *hail!*

báðir (báðar, bæði), ad. *both.*
band (-s, bönd), n. *bond, fetter.*
bann (-s, bönn *rare*), n. (*ban*) *prohibition; curse.*
banna (-aða, at.) v. a. *to forbid.*
bannaðr (bönnut, bannat), pp. *forbidden.*
bannsettr, pp. *accursed.*
barn (-s, börn), n. *a child.*
bauð, 1 and 3, past ind. of bjóða.
beiða (-dda), v. a. *to bid, ask, implore.* 2, *to demand, exact.*
beimi (-a, ar), m. *a man.*
bein (-s, id), n. *a bone.*
bera (ber, bar, bárum, bæri, borit), v. a, and n. *to bear, carry;* b. af

to excel; b. fram *to give forth, to utter;* b. í *to smear, anoint;* berr mik þar til ván *hope carries me thitherward, that is my hope;* henni bæri til fögnuð þenna (an ungrammatical phrase, probably because the preceding line has dropped the subject) *to her such joy were brought.*

bergja (-ða, -t), v. a. *to taste.*

berr, ad. *bare, naked.*

betri, comp. of góðr.

bifast, refl. of bifa *to quiver, to tremble, quake.*

binda (bind, batt, bundum, byndi, bundit), v. a. *to bind, fetter.*

bíta (bít, beit, bitum, biti, bitit) v. a. (*to bite*) *to eat.*

bitr, ad. *sharp.*

bjarga (-aða, -at), v. a. *to save;* b. sèr *to save one's self.*

bjartr (björt, bjart), ad. *bright.*

bjóða (býð, bauð, buðum, byði, boðit), v. a. *to offer;* b. sik fram *se offerre.*—2, *to command.*

bjúgr, ad. *bowed, bent down, humble; coiled.*

blanda (-aða, at), v. a. *to blend, to mix.*

blandinn, pp. *mixed.*

blárr, ad. *blue.*

blásinn, pa. *blown up, swollen.*

blástr (-rs, -rar), m. *breath.*

blekkja (-ta, -t), v. a. *to blacken, tarnish, soil, corrupt.*

blessaðr (blessuð, blessat), ad. *blessed.*

blíða (-u,–), f. *sweetness; delight.*

blíðr, ad. (*blithe*), *soft, gentle, sweet, mild.*

blinda (-aða, -at), v. a. *to blind.*

blindr, ad. *blind.*

blóð (-s,–), n. *blood.*

blóm (-s,–), n. *blossom, flower, fruit.*

blómi (-a, -ar), m. *bloom;* Maríu blómi *Mary's bloom, Christ.*

blóstr (-s and blóstrar), m. *breath.*

blót (-s,–), n. *sacrifice.*

blý-varða, f. *lead-bar.*

boð (-s,–), n. *bidding, command.*

boðorð, n. *commandment.*

bók (bókar, bœkr), f. (*beech*) *a book.*

borg (-ar, -ir), f. (*burgh*) *in* borgarmúr *guarding wall* (fig.)

brá, 1 and 3 past ind. of bregða.

brá (-ða, -ð), v. n. *to vibrate, twinkle, glimmer, glitter.*

bragð (-s, -brögð), n. *trick, wile, fraud.*

bragnar, m. pl. *men.*

brandr (-s, -ar), m. *brand, rod.*

bráðr, ad. *quick, swift;* neut. as adv. *quickly, swiftly.*

braut, prop. acc. sing. of braut = *road;* used as an adv. with usually an á before it, *abroad, off.*

bregða (bregð, brá, brugðum, brygði, brugðit), v. a. *to turn; alter, change;* b. til hætti *to turn, change the mode* (*of creation*).

breiða (-dda, -tt), v. a. *to spread out, to stretch.*

brenna (-da, -t), v. a., *to burn, urere.*

brenna (brenn, brann, brunnum, brynni, brunnit), v. n., *to burn, ardere.*

bresta (brest, brast, brustum, brysti, brostit), v. n. *to burst, break.*

breyta (-tta, -tt), v. a. *to change, alter.*

brigzl, n. *taunt, gibe, scoff.*

bringa (-u, -ur), f. (*brisket*), *breast, bosom.*

brjóst (-s,–), n. *breast.*

brjótr (-s, -ar), m. *breaker,* in synda-brjótr.

broddr (-s, -ar), m. *a spike, prick.*

brúðr (-ar, -ir), f. (*a bride*), *maiden, woman, lady.*

brugga (-aða, at), v. a. *to brew.*

brunnr (-s, -ar), m. (*burn*), *a well, fountain.*

brýndr, ad. *whetted, sharpened.*

búinn, pp. *ready; furnished with, fraught with.*

búkr (-s, -ar), m. *body, trunk.*

bundinn, pp. *bound.*

burðr (-ar,–), m. *birth.*

burt, adv. *away.*

býðr, *see* bjóða.
bygð (-ar, -ir), f. *abode.*
byggja (-ða, -t), v. n. *to abide, dwell.*
bylja-kast, n. *gusts of wind, figurative of storms of passion.*
bylr (-s, -ir), m. *a gale, sudden violent wind.*
byrgja (-ða, -t), v. a. *to wall up, hem in, cover, hide, close;* b úti *to shut out.*
byrgðr, pp. *hemmed in.*
bæði, adv. *both.*
bœn (-ar, -ir), f. *a boon, prayer.*
bæri, *see* bera.
bœta (-tta, -tt), v. a. *to boot,* b. um. *to intercede, redress.*
böl (-s, dat. bölvi), n. *bale, curse, misery.*
börn, *see* barn.

dáð (-ar, -ir), f. *deed; good, excellent work.*
dagligr, ad. *daily.*
dagr (-s, -ar), m. *a day.*
danskr (dönsk, danskt), ad. *Danish.*
dapr (döpr, daprt), ad. *faint, dim.*
dár (-s,–), n. *delusion, infatuation.*
daufr, ad. *deaf.*
dauði (-a,–), m. *death.*
dauðr, ad. *dead.*
deila (-da, -t), v.a. *to deal, divide; contest, strive.*
detta (dett, datt, duttum, dytti, dottit), v.n. *to fall, stumble;* d. á, *to fall upon, overtake.*
deyja, (dey, deyði and dó, dóum, dœi, dáit), v.n. *to die.*
díki (-s, id), n. *ditch, slough, pit.*
diktr (-s,–) m. *a poem.*
dikta (-aða, -at), v. a. *to compose in verse; to devise, scheme.*
diktan (-ar, -ir), f. *composition in verse.*
djöfla-bygð *the devils' abode.*
djöfla-díki *the devils' pit.*
djöfull (-s, -djöflar), m. *the devil.*
djúpleikr (-s,–), m. *depth, deep.*
dómr (-s, -ar), m. *doom, judgment, award.*
dóttir (-ur, dœtr), f. *daughter.*
draga (dreg, dróg, drógum, drœgi, dregit), v.a. *to drag, to draw.*
dráp (-s, id), n. *slaying, slaughter.*
drápa (-u, -ur), f. *a song on the slain ones; a laudatory, encomiastic poem.*
dreggjar, f. pl. *dregs.*
dreifa (-ða, -t), v.a. *to spread out, scatter, besprinkle, anoint;* refl. *to spread, or drift apart from one another.*
drengr (-s, ir), m. *a boy, fellow.*
drep (-s,–), n. *mortification, gangrene, deadliness.*
drepa (drep, drap, drápum, dræpi, drepit), v.a. *to smite, slay, kill.*
dreyri (-a,–), m. *blood (flowing).*
dreyrugr, ad. *bloody.*
drif (-s,–), n. *drift.*
drjúgr, ad. in the ellipt. dat. drjúgum, *fast, quickly, rapidly.*
dropi (-a, -ar), m. *a drop.*
drottinn and dróttinn (-s, drottnar), m. *a lord; the Lord.*
drottna (-aða, -at), v. a. *to sway, to rule.*
drottning (-ar, -ar), f. *a queen.*
drukkna (-aða, -at), v. inchoat. n. *to get drowned.*
drukknan (-ar -ir), f. *drowning.*
dúfa (-u, -ur), f. *a dove.*
duft (-s,–), n. *dust.*
duga (-ða, at), v. a. *to suffice, succour.*
duldr (for duliðr = dulinn), pp. *hidden;* d. em ek *res mihi celatur.*
dumbr, ad. *dumb.*
dvelja (dvel, dvaldi, dvöldum, dveldi, dvalit), v.n. *(to dwell), to stay, impede, trammel.*
dygð (-ar, -ir), f. *faith, faithfulness, virtue.*
dygðugr, ad. *virtuous.*
dyggleikr (-s,–), m. *faithfulness.*
dylja (dyl, duldi, duldum, dyldi, dulit), v. a. *to hide, conceal.*
dýr (-s, id), n. *(deer), beast, animal.*
dýrð (-ar,-), f. *glory;* d. englanna *the glory of the angels, God.*
dýrðar-menn *glorious lords.*
dýrr, ad. *dear, mighty, glorious.*
dœmi (-s, id), n. *example.*
dœgr (-s, id), n. *day and night.*

döggva (döggða, döggvat), v. a. *to bedew, besprinkle.*
dökkr, ad. *dark, gloomy, murky, swarthy.*

eð, another form of the relative er.
eða, adv. *or.*
edda (-u, -ur), f. *the Edda*; eddu regla *ancient eddaic rules for artificial and allegorical poetry.*
ef, adv. *if.*
efla (-da, -t), v.a. (afl) *to strengthen, to bring about.*
efna (-da, -t), v. a. *to fulfil, keep (a commandment).*
efri, comparat. from the root of, *higher.*
efstr, superl. from the same root, *highest.*
eftir, prep. with dat. and acc. *after;* adv. in leita eftir *to search for, implore;* eftir mest en þó er (al. fer) at lesti *that is yet the most, the worst, which follows sin.*
efunarlaust, n. ad. as adv. *without doubt or hesitation, see* ifunarlaust.
ei and eigi, adv. *not.*
eiðr (-s, -ar), m. *an oath.*
eign (-ar, -ir), f. *ownership; possession.*
eilíflega, adv. (ei [= aye], líf), *eternally.*
einberni, n. (barn), *one-begotten child.*
einfaldr (-föld, -falt), ad. *onefold, simple, plain.*
eingetinn, ad. *one-begotten, only-begotten.*
einhverr (einhver eitthvat and eitthvert), pron. indef. *someone, somewhat;* eitthvert sinni *some time.*
eining (-ar, -ar), f. *oneness, unity.*
einka-, in compounds, *only.*
einn (ein, eitt), card. num. *one.*
eisa (-u, -), f. *embers.*
eitthvat, *see* einhverr.
eitr (-s,–), n. *poison, venom.*
ek, gen. mín, dat. mèr, acc. mik, pl. nom. vèr (dual. við), gen. vor (d. okkar), dat. and acc. oss (d. okkr). *I, we (we both).*
ekki, adv. *not.*
ekki, neut. pron. *see* enginn.

eldr (-s, -ar), m. *fire.*
elska (-u,–), f. *love.*
elska (-aða, -at), v. a. *to love.*
elskandi (in þú ert e. ein af sprundum) pa. in a passive sense, *amandus.*
em and emk, 1 pers. s. pres. ind. of vera.
en, adv. *but, sed.*
engill (-s, englar), m. *an angel.*
enginn (engin, ekki; einn and the negat. gi), pron. indef. *no one, none.*
engla-rásir *streams, strings, hosts of angels.*
engla-stètt *angel station or order.*
enn (1), adv. *still, yet.*
enn (2), adv. *than.*
enn (3), def. art. = hinn.
enni (-is, id), pl. *forehead.*
epli (-is, id), n. *an apple.*
er (1), 1 and 3 sing. pres. ind. of vera.
er (2), pron. rel. indecl. *who, which, that, as.*
erindi (-s, id), n. *an errand, embassy.*
eyðing (-ar,-), f. *destruction.*
eymd (-ar, -ir), f. *misery, wretchedness.*
eyrindi = erindi.

fá (fæ, fèkk, fengum, fengi, fengit), v. a. *to get, obtain.*
faðir (föður, feðr), m. *a father.*
faðma (-aða, -at), v. a. *to embrace.*
faðmr (-s, -ar), m. *fathom, bosom.*
fagna (-aða, -at), v. a. (cp. *to fawn*), *to rejoice.*
fagnaðar-laug *tears of joy.*
fagr (fögr, fagrt), ad. *fair, beautiful.*
fái, *see* fá.
fáir, nom. pl. of fárr.
falla (fell, fèll, fèllum, fèlli, fallit), v. n. *to stumble, fall, drop.*
fann, *see* finna.
fár (-s,-), n. *plague, calamity, ruin.*
fara (fer. fór, fórum, fœri, farit), v.n. *to fare; to go.*
fárr (fá, fàtt), ad. *few.*
fasta (föstu, föstur), f. *a fast.*
fastr (föst, fast), ad. *fixed; fast;* neut. as adv. *vehemently.*

fátt, *see* **fárr**.
fátalaðr, ad. *few-spoken, of few words.*
fáviss, ad. *few-wise, unwise, foolish.*
feðgin, n. indecl. 1, *father and daughter* (cpr. v. 9, where the violence is personified as the devil's daughter tormenting him in everlasting fire); 2, *parents.*
fegurð (-ar-), f. *fairness, beauty.*
feikn (-ar, -ir), (A–S fácen ?) f. *hugeness, immensity, excess.*
feikr (feik, feikt), ad. *immense, excessive, monstrous.*
fèkk, *see* **fá**.
fela (fel, fal, fálum, fæli, falit), v. a. *to hide, conceal.*
fella (-di, -t), v. a. *to fell, throw over.*
feldr, pp. of fella, *felled, overthrown.*
fengi, *see* **fá**.
fengit, *see* **fá**.
ferð (-ar, -ir), f. *faring, travelling,* hence *flock, multitude; mankind.*
ferr, *see* **fara**.
festa (-ta, -t), v. a. *to fix;* refl. *to become fixed, inveterate.*
feta (fet, fat, fátum, fæti, fatit), v. n. *to step.*
fimm, num. card. *five.*
finna (finn, fann, fundum, fyndi, fundit), v. a. *to find; feel; to contrive.*
firr, adv. *far, afar.*
firra (-ða, -t), v. a. *to remove from; to deprive of;* refl. *to shun, avoid.*
fiskr (-s, -ar), m. *fish.*
fjall (-s, fjöll), n. (*fell*) *a mountain.*
fjandi (-a, fjandr and fjendr), m. 1, *foe;* 2, *the fiend.*
fjórir (fjórar, fjögr), num. card. *four;* fjórum einum *four only.*
fjúk (-s,–) n. prop. *snowdrift with a gale, figurative of the stormy nature of passion.*
fjöðr (fjaðrar, fjaðrir), f. *a feather.*
fjölkunnigr, ad. *astute, subtle.*
fjöturr (-s, fjötrar), m. *fetter.*
fleinn (-s, -ar), m. *a rod, sting, goad.*
flekklauss, ad. *spotless.*
flekkr (-s, -ir), m. *spot.*
flekkun (-ar-), f. *defilement, corruption.*
flengja (-da, -t), v. a. *to flog.*
flestr, *see* **margr**.
fljóta (flýt, flaut, flutum, flyti, flotit), v. n. *to flow, run.*
fljúga (flýg, flaug, flugum, flygi, flogit), v. n. *to fly.*
flóa (aða, -at), v. n. *to flow, flood.*
flóð (-s,–), n. *flood.*
flokkr (-s, -ar), m. *a flock, host.*
flýja (flý, flýða, flýðum, flýði, flýit), v. n. *to flee.*
flýta (-tta, -tt), v. a. in flýtandi *urging to hasten.*
flytja (flyt, flutta, fluttum, flytti, flutt), v. a. *to move from one place to another,* in oss er flutt *nobis traditum est.*
flærð (-ar, -ir), f. *guile, artifice, deceit.*
flærðarfullr, ad. *full of* flærð.
fold (-ar, -ir), f. (*field*) *earth.*
fólk (-s,–), n. *folk, people.*
fór *see* **fara**.
forðast, v. refl. (of forða), *to heed, shun, avoid.*
forðum, adv. *of yore.*
forma (aða, -at), v. a. *to form.*
forn, ad. *old, ancient.*
fórn (-ar, -ir), f. *offering, sacrifice.*
fornyrði, n. pl. *archaism.*
forvitni, f. *curiosity, inquisitiveness, pertness.*
foss (gen. like nom. but rare, -ar), m. *a force* (also written and pronounced *foss* in the North, *see* Halliwell); *a waterfall, torrent.*
fótr (-ar, fœtr), m. *a foot.*
frá, prep. with dat. *from, off.*
fram, adv. *forth, onward.*
frammi, adv. *forth, before, in front, coram.*
framr (fröm, framt), ad. *bold, pert.*
frásögn (-sagnar, -sagnir), f. *relation, record.*
freista (-aða, -at), v. a. with gen. *to try, to tempt, to beguile.*
frelsari, (-a–), m. *the Saviour.*
frelsi (-is,–), n. *freedom.*
fremd (-ar, -ir), f. *fame, honour.*
fremdarsnauðr, ad. *stripped of honour.*

frètta (-tta, -tt), v. a. *to ask, inquire, to learn by inquiry;* f. at *to inquire after.*
friðar-samband, n. *bond of peace.*
friðr (-ar,–), m. *peace.*
fríðr, ad. *fair, beautiful.*
frjáls, ad. *free.*
frost and fróst (-s, id.), n. *frost:* fig. *cold selfishness.*
frú (-ar, contr frùr, pl. frúr), f. *lady.*
frœði, n. pl. *lore.*
frægr, ad. *famed, glorious.*
fugl (-s, -ar), m. *fowl, bird.*
fúll, ad. *foul.*
fullr, ad. *full;* fullum hætti, *fully, rightwise.*
fundinn, pp. *found.*
fúss, ad. *willing, yearning, eager.*
fýla (-u,–), f. *foulness.*
fylgd (-ar, -ir), f. in fylgdar-menn, *followers.*
fylla (-da, -t), v. a. *to fill;* refl. *to fill, to abound with.*
fyrðar, m. pl. *folk, people.*
fyrir, prep. with dat. and acc. *for;* 1, with dat. *for, before, coram;* f. ásjó þinni; f. barni þinu &c.; *for, for the good of, on behalf of,* bœnarmál f. kristnum sálum. 2, with acc. *for, through* f. umsján þína; *for, by:* f. Maríu faðminn dýra; *for, in return for, in consequence of:* f. ódygð slíka, &c.
fyrirbjóða (bjóða), v. a. *to forbid.*
fyrirdœma (dœma), *to condemn, fordo.*
fyrirláta (láta), v. a. *to forgive.*
fyrirlíta (líta), v. a. *to scorn.*
fyrnska (-u, -), f. *old age, decrepitude.*
fyrri, comp. ad. *former; first.*
fyrstr, superl. ad. *first, foremost;* í fyrstu or simply fyrstu (dat. neut.) *at first, in the beginning.*
fýsa (-ta, -t), v. a. *to urge on;* refl. fýsask, id.; impers. mik fýsir, *I yearn.*
fœða (-dda, -tt), v. a. *to bear, give birth to;* refl. *to be born.*
fœddr, pp. *born.*
fældr, pp. *scarred.*
fœra (-ða, -t), v. a. *to move, bring;* refl. *to move one's self, draw;* f. nær *to draw nigh.*
fœra-glöggr, ad. *clear-sighted in seizing upon, watchful of, opportunities.*
fœri (-is id), n. *opportunity.*
fœrr, ad. *hale, alert.*
fæstir, *see* fárr.
fættast (fár), v. refl. *to diminish in strength or number.*
föðr-ætt, f. *father-kin.*
föðr-persona *the Father's person.*
fögnuðr = fagnaðr.
fölna (-aða, -at), v. inch. n. *to grow wan, wax pale.*
fölr, ad. *pale, wan.*
föra = fœra.
föstu, *see* fasta.
föstu-móðr, ad. (*mithered*), *weary with fasting.*

gaf, *see* gefa.
gáfa (-u, -ur), f. *gift, endowment.*
gall (-s,–), n. *gall, bile, rancour.*
gat, *see* geta.
gefa (gef, gaf, gáfum, gæfi, gefit), v. a. *to give.*
gegn, adv. *against.*
gegnum, adv. *through.*
geisli (-a, -ar), m. *a beam.*
gerr, pp. *made.*
geta (get, gat, gátum, gæti, getat), v. a. *to afford, to be able to;* impers. *to be got, obtained, found;* hvar getr þann er sèr megi bjarga *where may he be found who,* &c.
geyma (-da, -t), v. a. *to keep, guard, watch.*
geysa (-aða, at), v. a. (*to gush*), *to rush, roar* (*of fire*).
gift (-ar, -ir), f. *a gift.*
gifta (-u, -ur), f. *gift, good fortune.*
giftast (gifta *to give in marriage*), refl. *to wed.*
giftu-vegr, m. *way of good hap, via felicitatis.*
gildr, ad. *big, mighty, magnificent.*
gimsteinn, m. *a gem.*
gjafir, *see* gjöf.

gjalda (geld, galt, guldum, gyldi, goldit), v. a. *to yield, give, deliver, proffer.*
gjarna, adv. *readily, willingly, eagerly, (yearningly).*
gjöra (-ða, -t), v. a. *to make, shape, create; to do.*
gjörð (-ar, -ir), f. *deed, doing, making, work.*
gjörðr, pp. *made, shapen.*
gjörvallr (allr.), ad. *whole, complete, entire.*
glaðr (glöð, glatt), ad. *glad, joyful.*
gleði, f. ind. *gladness, joy.*
gleðiligr, ad. *gladdening, delightful; happy, gladsome, joyful.*
gleðja (gleð, gladdi, glöddum, gleddi, glatt), v. a. *to gladden;* refl. *to become glad.*
gler (-s, id.), n. *a glass.*
gleyma (-da, -t), v. a. *to forget.*
gleyming (-ar,–), f. *that whereby one forgets.*
glíking (-ar, ar), f. *likeness.*
glóa (-aða, -at), v. n. *to glow, to shine.*
glœpr (-s, -ir), m. *sin, vice, crime.*
glœsiligr, ad. *shining, beaming, bright.*
glöggr, ad. *clear, plain, distinct; keen, shrewd, clear-headed.*
gnísta (-ta, -t), v. a. *to gnash;* g. tennr *to gnash, grind one's teeth.*
Goð = Guð.
góðr, ad. *good.*
grafa (gref, gróf, grófum, grœfi, grafit), v. a. *to dig, bury.*
grand (-s, grönd), n. *hurt, ruin.*
granni (-a, -ar), m. *a neighbour, fellow, comrade.*
gráta (græt, grèt, grètum, grèti, grátit), v. a. and n. *to greet, weep, cry.*
grátinn, ad. *lacrimosus.*
grátr (-s,–), m. *weeping, crying.*
gras (-s, grös), n. *grass.*
greiðr, ad. *expedite, easy, quick.*
grein (-ar, -ir), f, *branch; division; distinction; batch* in sjö daga grein.
greina (-da, -t), v. a. *to distinguish; to relate.*
grenja (-aða, -at), v. n. *to roar,* hence *to give loudly vent to internal fury.*
grimd (-ar,–), f. *grimness, savageness, cruelty, fury, rage.*
grjót (-s,–), n. collect. *(grits), stones.*
grund (-ar, -ir), f. *ground, earth.*
grunnr (-s, -ar), m. *ground, bottom;* af grunni *from the bottom.*
grœða (-dda, -tt), v. a. *to heal, make whole.*
græðgi, f. ind. (gráð), *greed.*
grœðing (-ar,–), f. *healing.*
grœnn, ad. *green.*
grönnum, *see* granni.
Guð (-s), *God.*
guðdómr (dómr), m, *godhead.*
gull (-s, id.), n. *gold.*
gumi (-a, -ar), m. *a man.*
gæfi, *see* gefa.
gægjast, refl. *to peep, to pry.*
gæta (tta, -tt), v. a. *to heed, guard, watch.*

hafa (hef, hafða, höfðum, hefði, haft), v. a. *to have;* auxiliary and n. *to have.*
hagl (-s, högl), n. *hail.*
hagligr, ad. *shapely, comely; deft.*
hagleikr (-s,–), m. *deftness.*
halda (held, hèlt, hèldum, hèldi, haldit), v. a. *to hold, keep;* h. hátíð *to keep a festival.*
háleitr, ad. *high, sublime; elevated, majestic.*
háls (-s, -ar), m. *neck.*
hanga (hangi, hèkk, hèngum, hèngi, hangit), v. n. *to hang.*
hann (gen. hans, dat. honum, acc. hann; nom. pl. þeir, gen. þeirra, dat. þeim, acc. þá), 1, pron. third pers. *he.* 2, def. art. *the;* hann fjandi *the fiend.*
hár (-s, id.), n. *hair.*
harðr (hörð, hart), ad. *hard.*
harmr (-s, -ar), m. *grief, sorrow.*
hárr, ad. *high.*
hátíð (tíð), f. *feast, festivity.*
hauðr (-s,–), n. *earth.*
hefði, hefi, hefir, *see* hafa.
hefja (hef, hafða, höfðum, hefði,

hafit), v. a. *to heave aloft, to lift up; to begin, take origin.*
hefnd (-ar, -ir), f. *revenge.*
heiðingi (-ja, -jar), m. *a heathen.*
heiðinn, ad. *heathen, pagan.*
heiðr, ad. *serene, bright.*
heiðr (-rs,–), m. *honour, glory.*
heiðra (-aða, -at), v. a. *to honour.*
heilagr (heilög, heilagt), ad. *holy, sacred.*
heill, ad. *sound, hale well; whole, entire.*
heilsa (-u,–), f. *health.*
heimr (-s, -ar), m. (*home*), *the world.*
heims-stýrandi, m. *world-ruler.*
heim-leið (leið), f. *the homeward way.*
heita (heit, hèt, hètum, hèti, heitit), v. n. *to hight, to be called, to bear name.*
heitleiki (-a,–), m. *warmth.*
heitleikr (-s,–), m. id.
heitr, ad. *hot.*
heldr, adv. *but; on the contrary; rather, the more, far rather.*
helgr, adv. 1, *holy;* h. andi *the holy spirit.* 2, as a noun, *a saint.*
helstríð (stríð), n. *agony of death.*
helvíti (-s,–), n. *hell.*
hèr, adv. *here.*
herbergi (-is, id.), n. *harbour, room, apartment, dwelling.*
herðar, f. pl. *back (the shoulders and the part of the back which lies between them).*
herra (-a, -ar), m. *a lord, the Lord.*
hey (-s, dat. heyvi, id.), n. *hay.*
heyra (-ða, -t.), v. a. *to hear, listen, obey.*
himinn (-s, -nar), m. *the sky, the heaven (heavens).*
himna-ríki (ríki), n. *the kingdom of heaven.*
himneskr, ad. *heavenly.*
hingað, adv. *hither.*
hinn (hin, hit), def. art. *the.*
hinn (hin, hitt), pron. dem. *ille.*
hirð (-ar, -ir), f. *a court.*
hirðir (-is, -ar), m. *a herdsman.*
hitna (-aða, -at), v. inch. *incalescere.*
hitta (-tta, -tt), v. a. *to hit, find out.*
hjá, adv. *by.*
hjálp (-ar, -ir), f. *a help.*
hjálpa (-aða, -at), v. a. *to help; refl. to be holpen, to be saved.*
hjálpræði, n. *salvation.*
hjarn (-s, hjörn), n. prop. *a sheet of ice covering the snow, ice.*
hjarta (-a, hjörtu), n. *a heart.*
hlátr (-rs, -rar), m. *laughter.*
hlaupa (hleyp, hljóp, hlupum, hlypi, hlaupit), v. n. *to run.*
hljóta (hlýt, hlaut, hlutum, hlyti, hlotit), v. a. *to be obliged, forced, needs must.*
hlutr (-ar, ir), m. (*lot*), *a thing.*
hlýða (-dda, -tt), v. a. *to listen, to obey.*
hlýðinn, ad. *obedient.*
hlœgja (-ða, -t), v. a. *to make one laugh;* hlœgir mik at hèr muni teygjast, *it gives me joy that,* &c.
hnè (hnès, pl. id., gen. hnjáa, dat. hnjám), n. *a knee.*
hneigja (-ða, -t), v. a. *to bend, bow down, stoop.*
hold (-s, id.), n. *flesh.*
holdgan (-ar–), f. *incarnation.*
horskr, ad. *wise, sensible, endowed with knowledge and wits.*
hrapa (-aða, -at), v. n. *to tumble, slip down, fall.*
hreimr (-s,–), m. *many-voiced sound, noise.*
hreinferðugr, ad. *pure, chaste, righteous.*
hreinleikr (-s,–), m. *purity, chastity.*
hreinlífi, n. *chaste living; maiden purity.*
hreinn, ad. *pure, chaste; sincere.*
hreinsa (-aða, at), v. a. *to cleanse, to purify.*
hreistr (-s,–), n. *scales.*
hrekja (hrek, hrakta, hröktum, hrekti, hrakit), v. a. *to drive back, turn to flight, repel, vanquish.*
hrekkr (-jar, -ir), m. *trick, fraud, wile.*
hrella (-da, -t), v. a. *to grieve.*

hrista (-ta, -t), v. a. *to shake;* refl. *to tremble.*
hrjúfr, ad. *weak, decrepid; leprous?*
hróp (-s, id.), n. *cry, hooting.*
hryg𝔡 (-ar, -ir), f. *sadness, grief, affliction.*
hryggr, ad. *aggrieved, sad, afflicted; gloomy, awful.*
hræ𝔡ast, v. refl. *to fear, dread.*
hræddr, ad. *afraid, dreadful.*
hræ𝔡iliga, adv. *dreadfully.*
hræ𝔡sla (-u,–), f. *dread, fear.*
hrækja (-ta, -t), v. a. *to spit.*
hrœra (-𝔡a, -t), *to move, touch.*
hrœrandi, pa. *touching.*
hrœr𝔡r, pp. *devout, inspired; moved, changed.*
huga (-𝔡a, -at), v. a. and n. *to think about, apply one's thought to.*
hugr (-ar, -ir), m. *mind.*
hugsan (ar, -ir), f. *thought.*
huldr, pp. *hid, covered;* af huldu *in a hidden, secret wise.*
hulinn, ad. *hid, obscure, recondite.*
hús (-s, id.), n. *a house.*
hvat and **hva𝔡** (nom. and acc. neut. of a form. inus. hva, now hve), pron. indef. and interrog. *whatso; what?*
hválf (-s, id.), n. *a vault, a dome.*
hvar, adv. *where.*
hvekkr (-s and jar, -ir), m. *trick, fraud, deceit.*
hvergi, adv. *nowhere.*
hverr (hver, hvert, *gen.* hvers, hverrar, hvers, *dat.* hverjum, hverri, hverju, *acc.* hvern, hverja, hvert, *pl. nom.* hverir, hverjar, hver, *gen.* hverra, dat. hverjum, *acc.* hverja, hverjar, hver), pron. indef. and interr. *whoso, each one, who?*
hversu, adv. *how, how so.*
hví (prop. dat. of hvat), adv. *why.*
hvítr, ad. *white.*
hvorki, adv. *neither.*
hyggja (hygg, hug𝔡a, hug𝔡um, hyg𝔡i, hugat), v. a. and n. *to opine, think; to intend, to scheme.*
hylja (hyl, hulda, huldum, hyldi, hulit), v. a. *to cover, shroud; to hide, conceal.*
hæ𝔡 (-ar, -ir), f. *height,* himna hæ𝔡 *the high heavens.*
hæ𝔡a (-dda, -tt), v. a. *to mock, jeer, flout.*
hæddr, pp. *mocked,* &c.
hœgr, ad. *slow, soft, mild.*
hœgri, compar. of hœgr, *right,* h. hönd *the right hand.*
hærri, compar. of hárr.
hæstr, superl. of hárr.
höf𝔡ingi (-ja, -jar), m. *head, chief, master, lord.*
höfgi (-a, -ar), m. *heaviness, slumber.*
höfu𝔡 (-s, id.), n. *head.*
höfu𝔡-drottning, f. *regina princeps.*
höfu𝔡-engill, m. *archangel.*
höll (hallar, hallir), f. *a hall.*
hönd (handar, handir), f. *a hand;* til handa *for, on behalf.*

í, prep. with dat. and acc. *in, into.*
íbyggjari (-a, -ar), m. *inhabitant, dweller.*
i𝔡ran (-ar,–), f. *repentance.*
i𝔡r (-s, id.), n. *bowels; womb.*
ifunarlaust, adv. *without doubt or hesitation.*
illa, adv. *ill;* una i. *to be ill content at.*
illr (compar. verri, superl. verstr), ad. *ill, evil.*
ilmandi, ad. *fragrant, odorous, sweet.*
inn, adv. *into.*
inna (-ta, -t), v. n. *to express, utter;* i. til *to pray for;* refl. *to utter for one's self, to pray for (?);* innist ekki annat gott en af þèr til, Drottinn *nothing good can be uttered or prayed for, but what comes from thee, O Lord.*
innan, adv. *within.*
inni, adv. *within.*
innilegr, ad. *tender, beloved.*
innsigli (-s, id.), n. *seal.*
innstr, superl. *innermost.*
íturr, ad. *fair, stately.*

jafn (jöfn, jafnt), ad. *even, equal;* neut. jafnt, as an adv. *equally.*
jafnaldri (-ra, -ar), m. *equal in age.*
jafnan, adv. *commonly, invariably.*

jarðligr, ad. *earthly.*
jarðneskr, ad. *id.*
járn-hlið (hlið), *iron gates.*
játa (-tta, -at), v. a. and n. *to say yes, to confess, affirm.*
júngfrú (frú), f. *young lady, maiden.*
jörð (jarðar, jarðir), f. *the earth.*

kafna (-aða, -at), *to become smothered, suffocated, choked.*
kalla (-aða, -at), v. a. *to call; to claim.*
kanna (-aða, -at), v. a. (*to ken*), *to examine, explore, perscrutari*; refl. always with a við following it, *to become conscious of, to acknowledge.*
kast (-s, köst), n. *a throw*; bylja kast *a sudden dash of wind, procella.*
kátr, ad. *merry, gay.*
kenna (-da, -t), v. a. (*to ken*) 1, *to know*; pass. *to be known*, mátti Guðs þrenning með lýðum kennast *God's Trinity was to be known or seen among the people*; refl. *to acknowledge*, kennstu við svá at mín þú minnist; *to feel*: er ek kuldans kenni *when the cold I feel.* 2, *to teach*; kenn þú mèr at forðast fjandann *teach me to shun.*
kenning (-ar, -ar), f. *teaching, doctrine.*
keyra (-ða, -t), v. a. *to drive, strike.*
kind (-ar, -ir), f. (*kind*) *offspring.*
kinn (-ar, -ar), f. *cheek.*
kjaftr (-s, -ar), m. *a mouth, throat* (*of a wild beast*).
kjósa (kýs, kaus, kusum, kysi, kosit), v. a. *to choose.*
klókr, ad. *crafty, cunning.*
klæða (-dda, -tt), v. a. *to clothe, dress.*
klæddr, pp. *clothed, clad, dressed.*
klökkr, ad. *pliable, tender, contrite, humble.*
knè = hnè.
koma (kem, kom, kómum, kœmi, komit), v. n. *to come.*
konungr, kóngr, kúngr, kungr (-s, -ar), m. *a king.*
kostalauss, ad. *stripped of all good qualities, vile, evil.*
kraftr (-ar, -ar), m. *power, strength, might.*
kramdr (krömd, kramt), ad. *bruised.*
kreista (-ta, -t), v. a. *to squeeze, press.*
kremja (krem, kramdi, krömdum, kremdi, kramit), v. a. *to bruise.*
kringr (-s,–), m. *a circle, a round*; hence fig. in vèla-kringr, *insidiousness, astuteness, trickery*; í kring and í kring um *in a circle, in a circle around.*
kristinn, ad. *Christian.*
kristni, indecl. *Christendom.*
Kristr and Kristi (gen. Krists and Kristí, dat. Kristi, acc. Krist and Kristum), *Christ.*
krókr (-s, -ar), m. *a hook, crook, sting.*
kross (-id, -ar), m. *a cross, the cross.*
krossfesta, v. a. *to crucify.*
kúgaðr, pp. (*cowed*), *dismayed, prostrate.*
kuldi (-a, -ar), m. *a cold.*
kunna (kann, kunna, kunnum, kynni, kunnat), v. n. *to know* (*how to do*).
kunnigr, ad. *knowing, well up in; well known.*
kunnr, ad. *known.*
kvaddr, pp. *greeted.*
kvaldr, pp. *tormented, plagued.*
kváma (-u, -ur), f. *coming, arrival.*
kveðja (kveð, kvadda, kvöddum, kveddi, kvatt), v. a. *to greet, salute, accost, address.*
kveðja (-u, -ur), f. *greeting, &c.*
kvelja (kvel, kvalda, kvöldum, kveldi, kvalit), v. a. *to torment, plague.*
kvennmaðr, m. *a woman.*
kvíða (kvíð, kveið, kviðum, kviði, kviðit), v. a. and n. *to fear*; kv. við *to fear lest.*
kvíði (-a,–), m. *fear, anxiety.*
kvikr, ad. *quick, alive, living.*
kvistr (-s, -ir), m. *a sprig, twig, shoot, branch.*
kvittr (-s,–), m. *an inkling*; hence *aught* (*or nought*) *according to the context.*
kvæði (-is, id), n. *a poem.*

kvöl (kvalar, kvalir), f. *pain, plague, torment.*
kyrr, ad. *calm, quiet, tranquil.*
kyrrleikr (-s,–), m. *tranquillity, calm.*
kæra (-u, -ur), f. *accusation.*
kærr, ad. *dear to, beloved.*

laða (-aða, -at), v. a. *to invite, induce.*
lagast, refl. *to flow.*
lágraustaðr, ad. *of low voice.*
lamdr (lömd, lamit), pp. *beaten.*
land (-s, lönd), n. *a land.*
langr (löng, langt), ad. *long;* löngum, dat. pl. as adv. *long, by long whiles, always.*
langt, adv. loc. *far;* compar. lengra *further.*
lasta-vindr, m. *wind of vice, inflated passion.*
láta (læt, lèt, lètum, lèti, látit), v. a. *to let;* l. laust *to let loose;* l. sèr nœgja *to put up with;* refl. látast *to die.*
lauf (-s, id), n. *leaf, foliage.*
lauga (-aða, -at), v. a. *to bathe.*
lausnari, m. *Saviour.*
lausn (-ar, -ir), f. *loosening, release.*
leið (-ar, -ir), f. (load or lode), *way, road, path; journey.*
leiða (-dda, -tt), v. a. *to lead, bring.*
leiðar-nesti, n. (nesti), *load-fare, viaticum.*
leiðr, ad. *loathsome.*
leika (leik, lèk, lèkum, lèki, leikit), v. a. and n. *to play.*
leikr (-s, -ir), m. *a play.*
leiptr (-rs, id), n. *lightning.*
leita (-aða, -at), v. a. *to search, seek.*
leka (lek, lak, lákum, læki, lekit), v. n. *to drip, to drop.*
lemja (lem, lamda, lömdum, lemdi, lamit), v. a. *to beat, strike.*
lend (-ar, -ar), f. *loins.*
lengi, adv. temp. *long; comparat.* lengr *longer.*
lengra, *see* langt.
lesa (les, las, lásum, læsi, lesit), v.a. *to read.*
lèt, *see* láta.
letr (-s, id), n. *writing, record.*
lètta (-tta, -tt), v. a. and n. *to lighten, relieve; to abate, cease.*
lèttleikr (-s, -ar), m. *lightness, levity.*
lèttliga, adv. *easily.*
lèttr, ad. *light.*
leysa (-ta, -t), v. a. *to loosen, undo, free, save.*
líða (líð. leið, liðum, liði, liðit), v.n. *to glide; to pass; soar;* l. af. *to issue from; to depart from.*
líf (-s, –), n. *life.*
lifa (-ða, -at), v. n. *to live.*
lifandi, pa. *living, fresh.*
lífga (-aða, -at), v. a. *to enliven, to quicken.*
lífgan (-ar), f. *quickening.*
lífgari (-a, ar), m. *quickener.*
líflegr, ad. *lively, joyful.*
líf-þjónandi, pa. *ministering to life.*
líkami (-a, -ar), m. *body.*
líkamr (-s, ir), m. *id.*
líkja (-ta, -t), v. a. *to liken to;* líkjandi *comparandus;* refl. líkjast *to be like unto, to resemble.*
líkn (-ar, –), f. *mercy, compassion.*
líknar-vöndr, m. *mercy's rod.*
líknar-æðr, f. *vein, source of compassion.*
líkr, ad. *like.*
lilja (-u, -ur), f. *a lily.*
linhjartaðr, ad. *soft of heart.*
linni (-a, -ar), m. *a worm, snake.*
list (ar, -ir), f. *art, craft.*
listiligr, *see* lystuligr.
líta (lít, leit, litum, liti, litit), v. a. *to look; to behold;* refl. impers. mèr líst *meseems.*
lítillæti (is,–), n. *lowliness, humility, humbleness.*
ljóð, n. pl. *a lay, poetry.*
ljóða-gjörð, f. *lay-making, composing of poetry.*
ljós (-s, id.), n. *light.*
ljóss, ad. *light, bright; clear, perspicuous, evident.*
ljótr, ad. *ugly, lewd, wicked.*
lof (-s,–), n. *praise.*
lofa, (1) (aða, -at), v. a. *to leave, give leave, permit.*
lofa, (2) (-aða, -at), v.a. *to praise.*
lófi (-a, -ar), m. *the palm of the hand.*

lofligr, ad. *praiseworthy, adorable; full of praise.*
lofsöngr (-s, -var), m. *praiseful lays or songs.*
loft (-s, id.), n. *air, sky, heavens.*
logandi, pa. *flaming.*
lokka (-aða, -at), v. a. *to allure, entice, ensnare.*
luktr, pp. *closed.*
lúta (lýt, laut, lutum, lyti, lotit), v. n. (*to lowt*), *to bend, bow down, kneel down.*
lútr, ad. *bent, bowed down.*
lýðr (-s, -ir), m. *folk, people.*
lyftr, pp. *lifted up, raised.*
lygð (-ar, -ir), f. *a lying, i.e. nonsense, folly.*
lýsa (-ta, -t), v. a. *to lighten up, give light to.*
lyst (-ar, -ir), f. *lust, desire, appetite.*
lysta (-ta, -t), v. a. *to lust, desire, covet.*
lystiligr, ad. *desirable, enjoyable, delightful.*
lýta (tta, -tt), v. a. *to blemish; to throw blame upon, revile.*
lýti (-is, id.), n. *blemish, fault, defilement.*
lækning (-ar,–), f. *healing.*
lærisveinn (-s, -ar), m. *disciple.*
lögr (lagar, legir), m. *fluid; water (running or stagnant).*
löstr (lastar, lestir), m. *sin, vice, crime.*

má, *see* mega.
maðr (manns, menn), m. *a man.*
maklegleiki (-a, -ar), m. *desert, merit.*
makt (-ar,–), f. *might, power.*
maktr = máttkr.
mál (-s, id.), n. *speech.*
málmr (-s, -ar), m. *a metal.*
manndómr (-s,–), m. *mandom, manhood.*
manndráp (dráp), n. *manslaughter.*
mannvit (vit), *man-wit, human understanding.*
mánuðr and mánaðr (-aðar, -uðir, aðir), m. *a month.*
margbrugðinn, ad. *wily, subtle, astute.*
margfaldr (-föld, -falt), ad. *manifold.*
margfaldaðr, ad. id.
margr (mörg, margt), ad. *many.*
mátti, *see* mega.
máttkr (a contracted form for máttugr), ad. *mighty.*
máttr (-ar, mættir), *might, strength, power.*
með, prep. with acc. and dat. *with, in, by, through;* m. öllu *withal.*
meðan, adv. *while, whilst, awhilst.*
mega (má, mátti, máttum, mætti, mátt), v. n. *to may;* m. sèr ekki, *to be helpless;* líf þat er varð er mátti *a life which came when it might,* i.e. *in fit season.*
megn (-s,–), n. *main, might, power.*
meiða (-dda, -tt), v. a. *to hurt, harm.*
mein (-s, id.), n. *hurt, harm.*
meira, adv. *more.*
meiri, compar. of mikill.
meirr, compar. adv. *more.*
mekt (-ar, -ir), f. *might, power, strength.*
mektar-blóm (blóm), n. *flower of might.*
mektar-fullr. ad. *full of might.*
menniligr, ad. *human, incarnate.*
mèr, dat. sing. of ek.
merki (-is, id.), n. *mark, sign.*
merki-stjarna (stjarna), f. *star of the zodiacal signs (?), planet (?).*
mestr, superl. of mikill.
metnaðr (-ar,–), m. *pride, ambition.*
meydómr (-s,–), m. *maidenhood.*
meyja (-ar, -ar), f. *a may, maid, maiden, virgin.*
miðr (1) ad. *middle, midmost.*
miðr (2) (ð = nn, cpr. minnr), compar. adv. *less.*
mikill, ad. *mickle, great, large;* miklu, dat. sing. neut. as adv. *by a great deal.*
mildi, f. indecl. *mildness, pity, grace.*
mildr, ad. *mild, sweet, gracious, propitious, merciful.*
minka (-aða, -at), v. a. and n. *to lessen, diminish; to wane.*
minn (mín, mitt), ad. poss. *my, mine.*
minnast, v. refl. *to mind, remember, recollect;* m. á *to mention.*

minniligr, ad. *memorable.*
minnr, compar. adv. *less.*
miskunn (-ar,–), f. *pity, mercy, compassion.*
missa (-ta, -t), v. a. *to lose.*
mjólk (-ur,–), f. *milk.*
mjúkleikr (-s,–), m. (*softness*) *sweetness, comfort, grace.*
mjúkr, ad. *soft, smooth, sweet, gentle.*
móðerni, n. *maternity, kinship on the mother's side.*
móðir (-ur, mœðr), f. *a mother.*
móðr, ad. (*mithered*), *weary.*
móðr-mál (mál), n. *mother tongue, vernacular language.*
mold (-ar, -ir), f. *mould, earth.*
mund (-ar, -ir). f. *a hand.*
munnr (-s, -ar), m. *a mouth.*
munu (mun, munda, mundum, myndi,–), v. n. (*mon*) *shall, will.*
musteri (-is, id.), n. *temple.*
mynd (-ar, -ir), f. *form, figure, image.*
myndan (-ar, -ir), f. *formation.*
myrkr (-s, id.), n. *darkness.*
mýrr (-ar, -ar), f. (*moor*) *bog-land.*
mœðast, refl. of mœða *to weary, to get weary; to suffer.*
mæla (-ta, -t), v. a. *to speak;* vorðin (= orðin) svá at mælti forðum *the words which were spoken of old.*
mær (occurs only in nom. and vocat.), *a may, maiden, virgin.*
mætr, ad. *treasured, dear, beloved.*
mættag = mætta eg *I might; see* mega.
mætti, *see* mega.
mönde (= mundi), *see* munu.

ná (næ, náða, náðum, næði, náð), v. a. *to reach.*
náð (-ar, -ir), f. 1, *quiet, peace;* 2, *mercy.*
nagli (-a, -ar), m. *a nail.*
naktr (nökt, nakt), ad. *naked.*
nálgast, refl. *to draw nigh, approach.*
nálægr, ad. *nigh, near.*
náttúra (-u, -ur), f. *nature.*
nauð (-ar, -ir), f. *need, misery.*
nauðgr, ad. *unwilling, invitus.*
nauðsyn (-jar, -jar), f. *need.*
nè, conj. disjunct. *nor.*
neðri (compar. of the root neð, nið), *nether, lower.*
neðstr, superl. *nethermost, lowest, most infernal.*
nefna (-da, -t), v. a. *to name.*
nefndr, pp. *named.*
niðr, adv. *down;* n. um *adown.*
niðri, adv. *below.*
nista (-ta, -t), v. a. *to pierce.*
njóta (nýt, naut, nutum, nyti, notit), v. a. *to enjoy, derive benefit from;* látit mik þessa njóta þröngskorðaðra kvæðis orða *let these avail me, be of avail to me, stand me in good stead.*
nógr, ad. *sufficient; plentiful.*
nokkr, pron. ind. *some, some one, certain.*
nú, adv. temp. *now.*
nýjúng (-ar, -ar), f. *novelty, news.*
nœgja (-ða, -t), v. n. *to suffice.*
nœgr, ad. *sufficient, ample; exceeding.*
næsta, adv., prop. *nighest, nearest; much, exceedingly,* aldri var sá fyrr á foldu fœddur maðr ek næsta hræddumst *never was man amould born whom I dreaded nigh so much; well nigh,* jafnan hefi ek næsta kafnat *I have commonly been well-nigh drowned.*
nær, *see* ná.
nær, adv. *anigh.*
nærri, adv. *nigh;* n. nógu *well-nigh, near enough.*

óbreyttr, ad. *unchanged, unvaried; not involved, simple, plain.*
óbrunninn, pp. *unburnt.*
óðr, ad., prop. *mad; hence exceeding quickly repeated, rapid, frequent.*
óðr (-ar,–), m. *song, poetry.*
ódauðleikr (-s,–), m. *immortality.*
ódygð (-ar, -ir,), f. *unfaith, faithlessness.*
ofbeldi (-is,–), n. *violence, wantonness.*
offra (-aða, -at), *to offer sacrifice;* refl. *to offer one's self.*
offr (-s, id.), n. *offering, sacrifice.*
ofmetnoðr (-aðar,–), m. *over-ambition, exceeding pride, haughtiness, overbearing.*

ofrligr, ad. *exceeding, excessive.*
ofsi (-a,–), m. *wildness, fury, exceeding violence.*
oft, adv. temp. *oft, often.*
ógrátandi, pa. *unweeping, tearless.*
ok, conj. *and; (eke) also, too.*
oleusmurðr, pp. *anointed.*
óp (-s, id.), n. *cry, hooting.*
opinn, ad. *open.*
orð (-s, id., cpr. vorð), n, *a word.*
orða-hreimr, m. *wordy noise.*
orma-sveit (sveit), *worm hosts.*
ormr (-s, -ar), m. *a worm, serpent.*
oss, acc. pl. of eg.
óttandi, pa. *metuens*; from a verb, ótta, which does not occur in an intrans. sense, but which is still known in Iceland as a v. a.
ótti (-a,–), m. *fear.*
óvarlega, adv. *unwarily, heedlessly.*
overðugr, ad. *guiltless.*
óvinr (-ar, -ir), m. *unfriend, foe; the fiend.*
óvænn, ad. *desperate* (in objective sense); er óvænt stefndi *who steered a hopeless course, rushed headlong into destruction.*

páfugl (-s, -ar), m. *a peacock.*
pàlmi (-a, -ar), m. *a palm-tree.*
paradis (-ar, dat. paradísu,–), f. *paradise.*
paradisus, m. id.
past, n. *pastime.*
pentaðr, pp. *painted, radiant.*
pína (-u, -ur), f. *pain, passion.*
pína (-da, -t), v. a. *to torment*; refl. *to suffer on the cross.*
písl (-ar, -ir), f. *pain, passion, torment.*
píslàrfœri, n. *instruments of torture.*
plógr (-s,–), m. (*plough*) *produce of the earth.*
prettr (-s, -ir), m. *trick, fraud, wile.*
pressa (-aða, -at), v. a. *to press, squeeze; to drive on, propel.*
prísa (-aða, -at), v. a. *to praise.*
prófa (-aða, -at), v. a. *to try, make a trial; to prove.*
prýða (-dda. -tt), v. a. *to adorn, ornament.*
prýði, f. indecl. *ornament; beauty; glory*: p. umsníðingar *the beauty of circumcision*, i.e. *the beauty of the circumcisional ceremony.*

ráð (-s,– id.), n. *rede, counsel, advice, rule.*
ráða (ræð, rèð, rèðum, rèði, ráðit), v. n. *to follow one's own rede or counsel, have one's will*; v. a. *to rule.*
ráðlauss, ad. *unready, bewildered.*
rak, *see* reka.
rann, *see* renna.
rás (-ar, -ir), f. *string, stream* (*of living beings*), *see* engla-rásir.
rasa (-aða, -at), v. n. *to stumble, fare heedlessly.*
refsa (-aða, -at), v. a. *to punish.*
regla (-u, -ur), f. *rule.*
reiði, f. indecl. *wrath, anger.*
reifar, m. pl. *swaddle-cloth.*
reik (-s,–), n. *wandering, haunts.*
reika (-aða, -at), v. n. *to wander without an aim, to stray; to totter, reel, stagger.*
reikan (-ar,–), f. *uncertainty, hesitation, vacillation.*
reitr (-ar, -ir), m. *spot, region.*
reka (rek, rak, rákum, ræki, rekit), v. a. *to drive*; r. burt *to expel, chase away.*
remma (-u,–), f. *bitterness, corruption.*
remming (-ar,–), f. *strength, innate power*; r. hans ráða *the might of his counsel.*
renna (renn, rann, runnum, rynni, runnit), v. n. *to flow*; r. upp *to spring forth*; r. um *to flow, spread about.*
rètt, adv. *right, downright.*
rèttr, ad. *right, just.*
rèttferðugr, ad. *just, righteous, holy; proper, fit, suitable.*
rèttlátr, ad. *righteous, just.*
ríða (ríð, reið, riðum, riði, riðit), v. n. *prop. to ride; hence to fare impetuously*: kvíði ek við hans remming ráða ríði mèr at báðum síðum *timeo ne robur consiliorum ejus utrinque mihi impellatur.*

ríf**a** (ríf, reif, rifum, rifi, rifit), v. a. *to rive, tear.*
rigna (-di, -t), v. impers. *to rain.*
ríki (-s, id.), n. *realm, kingdom.*
ríkr, ad. *mighty, powerful.*
rísa (rís, reis, risum, risi, risit), v. n. *to rise.*
rjóðr, ad. *ruddy.*
roðnaðr (roðnut, roðat), ad. *reddened; ruddy.*
rós (-ar, -ir), f. *a rose.*
rósa (-u, -ur), f. id.
rœða (-dda, -tt), v. a. and n. *to speak;* r. um *to speak about.*
rœða (-u, -ur), f. *speech.*
rœgja (-ða, -t), v. a. *to libel; to revile.*
ræsir (-is,–), m. *a king.*
rödd (raddar, raddir), f. *a voice.*

sá (sú, þat, gen. þess, þeirrar, þess; dat. þeim, þeirri, því; acc. þann, þá, þat; nom. pl. þeir, þær, þau; gen. þeirra, dat. þeim, acc. þá, þær, þau), pron. dem. *that.*
sá, *see* sjá.
sál (-ar, -ir), f. *soul.*
samangaupnandi (gaupn = the hollow hands folded together), pa. *embracing.*
samangeypnandi, id.
samband (band), n. *bond, union, communion.*
samr (söm, samt), pron. dem. *the same, idem.*
samskínandi, pa. *shining together.*
samtengja (-da, -t), v. a. *to unite;* refl. *to become united.*
samvizka (-u, -ur), f. *conscience.*
sandr (-s, -ar), m. *sand.*
sanna (-aða, -at), v. a. *to prove, demonstrate.*
sannlega, adv. *verily, truly.*
sannr (sönn, satt), ad. *sooth, true, very.*
sár (-s, id.), n. (*sore*) *a wound.*
sárr, ad. *sore, wounded; painful.*
sat, *see* sitja.
saurgan (-ar,–), f. *pollution, defilement.*
sè, 1 sing. pres. subj. of vera.
sè, 1 sing. pres. ind. of sjá.
seggr (-s, -ir), m. *a man.*
seg, pres. imperat. of segja.
segja (segi, sagða, sögðum, segði, sagt), v. a. *to say.*
selja (-da, -t), v. a. *to sell.*
sem, pron. rel. indecl. *who, which, that, as.*
senda (-da, -t), v. a. *to send.*
sendiboði (-a, -ar), m. *messenger, ambassador.*
senn, adv. *soon; at once.*
sèr, dat. of sik.
sèr, 3 sing. pres. ind. of sjá.
sess (id. -ar), m. *seat.*
settr, pp. *placed; fixed; fraught with.*
sex, card. num. *six.*
síða (-u, -ur), f. *side;* s. lands *the border of the land.*
síðan, adv. *sithence, thereupon, afterwards.*
siðr (-ar, -ir), m. (*custom, manner*), *morals, good morals, righteousness.*
síðu-sár *side wound.*
signaðr, pp. *blessed.*
sigr (-rs, -rar), m. *victory, triumph.*
sigrandi, pa. *superans, excelling.*
sik (gen. sín, dat. sèr), pron. refl. se.
silfr (-s,–), n. *silver.*
sinn, poss. ad. *his, hers;* agrees with the object, never with the subject.
sinn (-s,–), n. *time.*
sinni (-is, -id), *id.*; at sinni *once;* sex at sinnum *six times;* eitthvert sinni *some time.*
sitja (sit, sat, sátum, sæti, setit), v. n. *to sit.*
sjá (sè, sá, sáum, sæi, sèð), v. a. *to see, behold.*
sjálfr, pron. dem. *self;* sjálft hreinlífit = *the very chastity.*
sjöfaldr, ad. *sevenfold.*
skaka (skek, skók, skókum, skœki, skekit), v. a. *to shake.*
skapa (-aða, -at), v. a. *to shape, to create.*
skapan (-ar,–), f. *creation.*
skapaðr, pp. *created.*
skapari (-a,–), m. *creator.*

skástr, superl. without a posit. *best.*
skaut (-s, id.), n. *sinus.*
skein, *see* skína.
skeina (-da, -t), v. a. *to wound.*
skepna (-u, -ur), f. *a creature;* s. öll *all created beings.*
skera (sker, skar, skárum, skæri, skorit), v. a. (*to shear*), *to cut.*
skeyti (-s, id.), n. *dart.*
skilja (-da, -it), v. a. 1, *to divide, sort;* s.˚undan *to leave out, forget.* 2, *to discern, understand.*
skilningr (-s,–), m. *understanding.*
skína (skínn, skein, skinum, skini, skinit), v. n. *to shine.*
skínandi, pa. *shining, bright, pure.*
skinn (-s, id.), n. *a skin; complexion.*
skírn (-ar, -ir), f. *baptism.*
skjálfa (skelf, skalf, skulfum, skylfi, skolfit), v. n. *to shake, tremble.*
skjótr, ad. *quick;* skjótt, adv. *quickly.*
skógr (-ar, -ar), m. *a wood, forest.*
skorða (-u, -ur), f. *a prop, stay,* (*wedge?*).
skorða (-aða, -at), v. a. *to prop, stay, steady.*
skrýða (-dda, -tt), v. a. *to attire stately;* refl. *to adorn one's self.*
skulu (skal, –, skyldi,–), v. def. *shall.*
ský (-s, id.), n. *a cloud.*
skygn, ad. *keen of sight; pellucid, transparent.*
skygnleikr (-s,–), m. *keenness of vision, pervading clearness.*
skylda (-u, -ur), f. *duty.*
skylda (-aða, -at), v. a. *to oblige, bind in duty;* refl. *to be obliged.*
skyldr, ad. *bound in duty.*
skynsemi, f. *reason, wit.*
skýra (-ða, -t), v. a. *to explain.*
skýrleikr (-s,–), m. *clearness.*
skýrr, ad. (*sheer*) *clear, pure, bright.*
skærleikr (-s,–), m. *brightness, radiance, purity.*
skær, ad. *pure, radiant, bright, pellucid.*
sköpun (-ar,–), f. *creation.*
slá (slæ, slòg, slógum, slœgi, slegit), v. a. *to strike, smite.*
slèttr, ad. *even, smooth, soft.*
slíkr, ad. *such.*
slíta (slít, sleit, slitum, sliti, slitit), v. a. *to tear.*
slúnginn, pp. *interwoven* (*artificial?*), *or wrought according to involved metrical rules.*
slœgð (-ar,–), f. *craft, wile, astuteness, subtlety.*
slœgr, ad. *astute, crafty, subtle.*
slœgvitr, ad. *of a wily mind.*
smán (-ar, -ir), f. *debasement, shame.*
smíða (aða, -at), v. a. (*to smithy*) *to shape, form, make.*
smyrsl, n. pl. *ointment, balm.*
snauðr, ad. *bereft, stripped of, poor.*
snerust, *see* snúa.
snild (-ar,–), f. *excellence, beauty, grace, charm* (*of speech, style, and the like*).
snilli, f. indecl. id.
snúa (sný, snera, snerum, sneri, snúit), v. a. *to turn, twist.*
snökta (-ta, -t), v. n. *to sob.*
sól (-ar, -ir), f. *the sun.*
sóma-örr, ad. *bountifully bestowing honours.*
sómi (-a,–), m. *honour, majesty.*
sonr (-ar, synir), m. *a son: the Son.*
sótt (-ar, -ir), f. *disease, plague, pain.*
spá (-ða, -ð), v. a. *to prophesy.*
spádómr (-s, -ar), m. *spaedom, prophesy.*
spádóms-orð, n. *words of prophecy.*
spenna (-ta, -t), v. a. (*to span*), *to stretch, to clasp.*
sphera, f. *sphere.*
spilla (-ta, -t), v. a. (*to spill, spoil*) *defile;* refl. *to become corrupt.*
sprund (-s, id.), n. *a woman.*
staðr (-ar, -ir). m. *stead, place, town;* halda stað *to abide.*
standa (stend, stóð, stóðum, stœði, staðit), v. a. *to stand.*
stanga (-aða, -at), v. a. *to sting, pierce;* stángast, pass. *to be stung.*
stef (-s, id.), n. *a stave* (?) *a strophe or half-strophe,* making a bar between any two portions of a stefja-drápa.
stefja-drápa, f. *a song containing* stefja-mál.
stefja-mál, n. pl. *stave-lay;* that por-

tion of a stefja-drápa which is divided by a stef from the fore part and the concluding part; in Lilja the stave-lay equals both these parts taken together in the number of its stanzas.
stefligr, ad. *which has in it a* stef.
stefna (-da, -t), v. n. *to go in a certain direction; to point; proceed.*
stefnligr (v. l. for stefligr), ad. *one who points to or moves in the right direction;* cpr. the modern óstefnuligr *madly rushing on.*
stètt (-ar, -ir), f. (*pavement*) *path; state, station; order.*
stilla (-ta, -t), v. a. *to moderate.*
stinnr, ad. *stiff, strong.*
stjarna (stjörnu, stjörnur), f. *a star.*
stjörnu-ljós, n. *starlight.*
stjörnu-reitr, m. *star region.*
stórmerki, n. *miracle.*
stormr (-s, -ar), m. *a storm; brunt.*
stórr, ad. *big, large, great.*
strengr (-s -ir), m. *a string, chord.*
stræti (-is, id.), n. *a street.*
stuðull (-s, stuðlar), m. *a stay, stayer, prop; main letters in the first line of every couplet.*
stund (-ar, -ir), f. *an hour, while, time.*
stunda (-aða, -at), v. a. *to study;* s. á *to pursue steadily a plan.*
stundum, *prop,* dat. pl. of stund, cpr. Engl. *whilom of while,* adv. *at whiles, now and then.*
styggja (-ða, -t), v. a. *to offend.*
stynja (styn, stunda, stundum, styndi, stunit), v. n. *to groan, to sigh.*
stýra (-ða, -t), v. a. *to steer, rule, govern.*
styrkr (-s,–), m. *strength, power, might.*
styrkr, ad. *strong, powerful, mighty.*
stökkva (stekk, stökk, stukkum, stykki, stokkit), v. n. (*to leap*) *burst, spout.*
sú, *see* sá.
sullr (-ar, -ir), m. *an ulcer.*
sundraðr (sundruð, sundrað), pp. *in sunder torn.*
súnginn, pp. *sung.*
sunnudagr, m. Sunday.
sút (-ar, -ir), f. *grief, sorrow.*
súta-myrkr, n. *gloom of sorrow.*
sút-hrœrandi, pa. *grief-promoting, heart-rending.*
svá, svo, adv. *so; thus.*
svar (-s, svör), n. *an answer.*
svara (-aða, -at), v. a. *to answer.*
svartr, ad. *swarthy.*
sveinn (-s, -ar), m. (*swain*) *a man-child.*
sveit (-ar, -ir), f. *a host.*
svella (svell, svall, sullum, sylli, sollit), v. n. *to swell.*
sverð (-s,– id.), n. *a sword.*
svíða (svíð, sveið, sviðum, sviði, sviðit), v. n. *to get singed, to burn.*
sviddu, 3 pl. part. ind. for sviðu.
sviðra (-aða, -at), v. n. *to singe the surface; to scorch.*
svíkja (svík, sveik, svikum, sviki, svikit), v. a. *to beuray, deceive, seduce.*
sýna (-da, -t), v. a. *to show.*
synd (-ar, -ir), f. *sin.*
synda-brjótr, *sin-breaker, Christ.*
syndga (-aða, -at), v. a. *to sin.*
syndrast, refl. *to become torn asunder.*
sýngja (sýng, söng, súngum, sýngi, súngit), v. a. *to sing.*
sýniligr, ad. *visible.*
sæla (-u,–), f. *bliss, beatitude.*
sœmd (-ar, -ir), f. *honour.*
sæti (-is, id.), n. *seat.*
sæti, *see* sitja.
sœtleikr (-s,–), m. *sweetness.*
sœtr, ad. *sweet.*
særa (-ða, -t), v. a. *to wound.*
sök (sakar, sakir), f. *cause.*
sökkva (-ta, -t), v. a. *to sink;* refl. *to sink, fall.*
söm, *see* samr.

Taka (tek, tók, tókum, tœki, tekit), v. a. and n. *to take; begin;* t. af *to abate, wane, dwindle, die away.*
tala (-aða, -at), v. a. and n. *to speak.*
tala (tölu, tölur), f. *tale, number.*
taldr, pp. *said.*
tapa (-aða, -at), v. a, *to lose, forfeit.*
tár (-s, id.), n. *a tear.*

tára-flóð, n. *flood of tears.*
telja (tel, taldi, töldum, teldi, talit), v. a, *to tell, count, calculate, guess at, consider.*
temja (tem, tamda, tömdum, temdi, tamit), v. a. (*to tame*) *to chastise.*
tènaðr (-ar,–), m. *favour, intercession.*
tendra (-aða, -at), v. a. *to enkindle;* refl. *to become enkindled.*
tennr, *see* tönn.
teygja (-ða, -t), v. a. (*to tug*), *to stretch out, expand; to entice, allure, beguile.*
tíðindi, n. pl. *news, events.*
tign (-ar,–), f. *dignity, honour, glory, majesty.*
tigna (-aða, -at), v. a. *to worship, adore.*
tignar-kveðja, f. *majestic greeting.*
til, prep. with gen. *to.*
tími (-a, -ar), m. *time.*
tíu, num. card. *ten.*
tjóa (-aða, -at), v. n. impers. *to do;* engum tjóar *it behoves no one.*
tól (-s, id.), n. *a tool, organ;* raddar tól *organs of speech.*
traust (-s,–), n. *trust; faith, confidence.*
trauðr, ad. *tardy, slow, unwilling;* trautt, n. as adv. *scarcely, barely, hardly.*
treysta (-ta, -t), v. a. *to trust, confide in;* refl. *to trust one's self, to find one's self able to.*
trú (-ar,–), f. *faith, belief; religion.*
trúa (-ða, -at), v. a. *to trow, believe;* trúi ek *methinks.*
túnga (-u, -ur), f. *a tongue.*
tvá acc. pl. of tveir.
tveir (tvær, tvö), num. card. *two, twain.*
tvennr, ad. *twofold, bini.*
tvisvar, adv. *twice.*
týna (-da. -t), v. a. (*to teen*) *lose.*
týndr, pp. *lost.*
typta (-aða, -at), v. a. *to chastise, correct.*
tœki, *see* taka.
tænaðr (-ar,–), m. =tènaðr.
tönn (tannar, tennr), f. *a tooth.*

údœmi, n. pl. *monstrosity.*
ugga (-ða,–), v. n. *to misdoubt, fear, apprehend.*
ugglauss, ad. *fearless, heedless.*
uggr (-s,–), m. *fear, apprehension.*
ull (-ar,–), f. *wool.*
um, prep. with acc. *of, about, round, through; as to.*
umbœta (-tta, -tt), v. a. *to aboot, atone for.*
umrennandi, pa. *revolving.*
umsján (-ar,–), f. *oversight, care.*
umsníðing (-ar,–), f. *circumcision.*
una (-da, -at), v. a. *to be content with;* u. illa við *to be ill content with.*
undan, adv. *from under; from, away;* skilja u. *to leave out;* víkja u. *to give place, cede.*
undarligr, ad. *wonderful, strange, singular.*
undirstaða (-stöðu, stöður), f. *fundament, principle.*
undrast, refl. *to wonder.*
úngr, ad. *young.*
unna (ann, unna, unnum, ynni, unnat), v. a. *to love, cherish.*
upp, prep. with acc., and adv. *up;* u. yfir *up above.*
upp-fœddr, pp. *fed on, brought up.*
upphaf (-s,–), n. *the upper ocean, the upper vast, firmament; beginning.*
uppi, adv. *up above.*
upprísandi, pa. *rising up again from the dead;* upprísöndum allra landa íbyggjurum *as the dwellers of all lands arise from the dead.*
út, adv. *out;* inna ú *to express.*
utan, adv. *except, outtaken.*
úti, adv. *out, without;* byrgja ú. *to exclude.*

vafðr, pp. *woven, twisted.*
vagna, *see* vakna.
vakna (-aða, -at), v. n. *to awake.*
vald (-s, völd), n. *power, might.*
valdr (-s, -ar), m. (*wealda*) *ruler.*
vanda (-aða, -at), v. a. *to work out elaborately.*
vandr, ad. *difficult, artificial.*
vann, *see* vinna.
vanr, ad. *wont, accustomed.*

vansi (-a,–), m. *shame, disgrace.*
varða (-aða, -at), v. a. *to ward, guard,* occurs only as impers. in Lilja: *it imports, it is necessary:* varðar mest til allra orða undirstaðan sè rèttlig fundin *therein is the greatest importance that the true meanings of the words be found;* mik varðar öllu *all lieth thereon for me.*
varkunnigr, ad. *short of knowledge, unskilled.*
varla, adv. *scarcely.*
varna (-aða, -at), v. a. *to ward off; to deny, refuse, with-hold.*
várr, varr, vórr, vorr, poss. ad. *our, ours.*
vatn (-s, vötn), n. *water; flood of tears.*
vátta (-aða, -at), v. a. *to witness, testify.*
váttr (-ar, -ar), m. *a witness, proof.*
vaxa (vex, óx, uxum, yxi, vaxit), v. n. *to wax, grow, increase.*
vefja (vef, vafða, vöfðum, vefði, vafit), v. a. *to weave, twist; to enfold.*
veggr (-s, -ir), m. *a wall.*
vegna (-aða, -at), v. n. *to fare, do.*
vegr (-ar, -ir), m. *a way, road, journey; honour, esteem.*
vegsamligr, ad. *worthy of worship, adorable, glorious.*
vegsemd (-ar,–), f. *honour, glory.*
veita (-tta, -tt), v. a. *to grant, give.*
veit, *see* vita.
vel, adv. *well.*
vèl (-ar, -ar), f. *wile, guile, craft.*
vèla-kringr *wily insidiousness.*
velja (vel, valda, völdum, veldi, valit), v. a. *to choose.*
velta (-ta, -t), v. a. *to roll;* refl. veltast *to roll, wallow, welter.*
veltiligr, ad. *voluble, revolving.*
vera (er, var, várum, væri, verit), v. n. *to be;* v. til *to exist, to be in reserve;* eitt er til *one thing is still to be resorted to.*
verð (-s, id), n. (*ward*), *price, reward.*
verða (verð, varð, urðum, yrði, orðit), v. n. *to grow, wax, become.*
verðugr, ad. *worthy, fit.*
verðleiki (-a, -ar), m. *merit, desert.*
verðleikr (-a, -ar), m. id.
verk (-s, id), n. *a work.*
verki (-a, -ar), m. (*ποίημα*), *what is wrought in rhyme, poetry, song.*
vernd (-ar, -ir), f. *protection.*
verndar-skaut, *see* skaut.
verri, comp. of illr.
vesall, or vesæll (ve neg. and sæll *blissful;* cpr. Lat. ve-sanus, contr. vesl), ad. *wretched, miserable, woful.*
við, prep. with dat. and acc. *with, by, against.*
víða, adv. *wide about, far and wide about.*
við-líkjast, refl. *to liken one's self to, to get, become like, unto.*
viðr (-ar, -ir), m. *wood, timber.*
víðr, ad. *wide, broad.*
viðrkenna (-da, -t), v. a. *to acknowledge, realize.*
viðrlíkjast = viðlíkjast.
víf (-s, id), n. *woman.*
vígja (-ða, -t), v. a. *to consecrate;* refl. vígjast, in a passive sense, *to be consecrated.*
víkja (vík, vèk and veik, vikum, viki, vikit), v. a. and n. *to turn;* v. at *to turn towards.*
vilja (-da, -at), v. a. *to will, desire.*
vilji (-a,–), m. *a will;* af vilja *on purpose;* vita at v. *to point towards a settled purpose.*
vinda (vind, vatt, undum, yndi, undit), v. a. *to wind, twist, twirl.*
vindr (-ar, -ar), m. *a wind;* vindi fult ofbeldi *inflated violence or passion.*
vinna (vinn, vann, unnum, ynni, unnit), v. a. (*to win*), *to work, labour, travail; to act; to commit; do;* v. til *to work for, deserve.*
virða (-ta, -t), v. a. *to price, value;* refl. virðast *to deem;* mèr virðist *meseems.*
virðar, m. pl. *men.*
virðing (-ar, -ar), f. *honour; honours.*

vísa (u, -ur), f. prop. *ditty; song, poem.*
víss, ad. *certain, sure;* n. víst as adv. *certainly.*
vist (-ar, -ir, in 13, 3, written víst), f. *dwelling, abode.*
vita (veit, vissa, vissum, vissi, vitat), v. a. *to know; to point towards.*
vitr, ad. *wise.*
vizka (-u,–), f. *wisdom.*
von (-ar, -ir), f. *hope.*
vorðin, 3, 6, = orðin, *see* orð.
vorkenna *to bear with, excuse.*
votta, *see* vátta.
vottr, *see* váttr.
vunninn, pp. = unninn of vinna.
vuxu, 3 imp. pl. ind. of vaxa.
vyrði = yrði, *see* verða.
vægð (-ar,–), f. *pity, compassion, mercy.*
vægja (-ða, -t), v. a. *to spare.*
vænast, refl. *to hope.*
vænta (-ta, -t), *to expect, hope.*
vætta (-tta, -tt), v. a. *to expect, hope.*
völundar-hús, n. *the house of Velent, a maze, a labyrinth.*
vör (varar, varir), f. *a lip.*
vörr (varrar, varrar), f. id.

yðr, dat. and acc. pl. of þú.
yðvarr (yður, yðvart), ad. poss. *your, yours.*
yfir-bjóðandi (-anda, -endr), m. *over-ruler.*
yfir-meistari (-a, -ar), m. *over-master, chief dispenser.*
yfir-morðingi (-ja, jar), m. *arch-murderer.*
yfir-spennandi (anda, -endr), m. *he who embraces.*
yfir-valdandi (-anda, -endr), m. *over-ruler, having the highest power over.*
yfrið, a form produced by crasis and radical vowel-change from the obsolete ofr, n. *a great thing,* and the art. hit or hið giving intensity to the sense = ofr hit, cpr. Engl. *much that;* prop. acc. sing.), adv. *right much, exceedingly, extremely.*

ykkr, dat. and acc. dual. of þú.
ykkvarr (ykkur, ykkvart), ad. poss. (σφωΐτεροι), *your, yours* (*of two*).
ýms, ad. *various.*
yndi (-is,–), n. *delight.*
ynnist, *corrupt reading for* innist.
yrkja (-ta, -t), v. a. (*to work*), *to compose poetry.*
ýtar, m. pl. *men.*

þá, adv. temp. *when;* þ. er *whenas.*
það, *see* sá.
þagna (-aða, -at), v. a. *to wax silent, become hushed.*
þakka (-aða, -at), v. a. *to thank.*
þangat, adv. loc. *thitherward,* temp. þ. til *till, until.*
þann, *see* sá.
þar, adv. loc. *there;* þ. sem *whereas;* þ. til *thereto.*
þat, conj. (*for* at), *that.*
þau, *see* sá.
þegar, adv. *when; forthwith, straightway.*
þeigi, *see* þeygi.
þeim, *see* sá.
þeirra, *see* sá.
þenna, *see* þessi.
þèr, *see* þú.
þessa, gen. pl. of þessi, in þ. þröngskorðaðra kvæðis orða.
þessi (þessi, þetta, gen. þessa, þessarrar, þessa, dat. þessum, þessarri, þessu, acc. þenna, þessa, þetta; pl. nom. þessir, þessar, þessi, gen. þessa and þessarra, dat. þessum, acc. þessa, þessar, þessi), pron. dem. *this.*
þeygi (= þó eigi), adv. *not at all, by no means.*
þið, *see* þú.
þik, *see* þú.
þín, *see* þú.
þína, *see* þinn.
þinn (þín, þitt, gen. þíns, þinnar, þíns, dat. þínum, þinni, þínu, acc. þinn, þína, þitt; pl. nom. þínir, þínar, þín, gen. þinna, dat. þínum, acc. þína, þínar, þín), ad. poss. *thy, thine.*

þjóð (-ar, -ir), f. *people, nation.*
þjóna (-aða, -at), v. a. *to serve;* þ. fyrir yðarn sóma *to serve for, minister to, thy Majesty.*
þjónn (-s, -ar), m. *servant.*
þjóstr (-s,–), m. *rancour, ill-will.*
þó, conj. *yet, though.*
þokki (-a,–), m. *favour.*
þola (-da, -at), v. a. (*to thole*), *bear, suffer, sustain.*
þótt (=þó at), adv. *although.*
þrangdr, pp. *oppressed* = þrengdr.
þrengdr, pp. *oppressed.*
þrenning (-ar,–), f. *Trinity.*
þrennr, ad. num. *threefold.*
þrettandi, num. ord. *the thirteenth.*
þriði, num. ord. *the third.*
þrisvar, adv. num. *thrice.*
þrítugr, ad. *of three tens;* á þrítugs aldri *at the age of thirty.*
þrúnginn, pp. *swollen, swelled.*
þrútinn, pp. id.
þræll (-s, -ar), m. *a thrall; an evil fellow.*
þrætugjarn, ad. *quarrelsome.*
þröng, f. *angustia, straits, jeopardy, want.*
þröngr, ad. *narrow.*
þröngskorðaðr (skorða), pp. *close-wedged or squeezed together.*
þú (gen. þín, dat, þèr, acc. þik; pl. nom. þèr, dual. þið, gen. yðar, d. ykkar, dat. and acc. yðr d. ykkr), pron. pers. *thou.*
þurfa (-ta, -t) v. n. *to need.*
þurftugr, ad. *needy.*
þverra (þverr, þvarr, þurrum, þyrri, þorrit), v. n. *to wane, dwindle away.*
því, prop. dat. neut. of sá, as adv. *therefore;* þ. at *because;* before comparatives, *the;* þ. miðr *the less.*
þvílíkr, ad. *such.*
þvínga (-aða, -at), v. a. *to oppress, force.*
þykkja (þykkir, þótta, þóttum, þœtti, þótt), v. impers. *to think, deem;* mèr þykkir *meseems;* refl. ek þykkjumst (=þykkjumsk for the older þykkjumk = þykkir mèr), *I think, feel.*
þyrnir (-is, -ar), m. *a thorn.*
þyrsta (-ta, -t), v. imp. *to thirst.*
þyrstr, ad. *thirsty.*
þökk (þakkar, þakkir), f. *thank;* in pl. *thanksgiving.*

æ, adv. *aye, always, ever, for ever.*
æðr (-ar,–), f. *a vein; a spring, source.*
æðri, comp. (of the root óð = áð in f. ex. áðr, &c.), *higher, nobler.*
æfi, f. ind. *lifetime, age;* um aldr ok æ. *through time and eternity.*
æfinlega, adv. *unceasingly; at all time, ever, for ever.*
œpa (-ta, -t), v. n. (*to whoop*), *to cry.*
æra (-u,–), f. *esteem, honour.*
œrinn, ad. *sufficient, sufficing.*
œrr, ad. *crazy, mad.*
æru-snauðr, ad. *bereft of honour, shamed.*
œsa (-ta, -t), v. a. *to rouse, urge, stimulate;* refl. œsask *to rush, to gush.*
œskja (-ta, -t), v. a. *to wish, desire, pray for.*
œstr, pp. *roused, violent, wanton, furious.*
ætt (-ar, -ir), f. *a family; generation.*
ætla (-aða, -at), v. a. *to have in the mind's eye, to intend, to purpose;* æ. sèr *to presume;* æ. undan *to be bent on an escape.*
œtti, 3 sing. imperf. ind. of œtta, v. n. (from ótti), *to fear* (?).
ætti, *see* eiga.

öðlast, refl. *to acquire, obtain, get possession of.*
öðru, *see* annarr.
öfund (-ar,-), f. *envy.*
öll, öllum, *see* allr.
önd (andar, andir), f. *spirit, soul.*
övunda (-aða, -at), v. a. *to envy.*

London: Strangeways and Walden, Printers, Castle St. Leicester Sq.